A SECRET CHRISTMAS

LAUREN ROYAL

A SECRET CHRISTMAS by Lauren Royal

Published by Novelty Books, a division of Novelty Publishers, LLC, 205 Avenida Del
Mar #275, San Clemente, CA 92674

COPYRIGHT © Lauren Royal 2017

Cover by Kimberly Killion

Learn more about the author and her books at www.LaurenRoyal.com.

ISBN: 1-63469-089-3

ISBN-13: 978-1-63469-089-8

ALSO BY LAUREN ROYAL

CHASE FAMILY SERIES

Amethyst

Emerald

Forevermore: A Chase Family Novella

Amber

Violet

Lily

Rose

A Secret Christmas

REGENCY CHASE FAMILY SERIES

Lost in Temptation

Tempting Juliana

The Art of Temptation

RENAISSANCE CHASE FAMILY SERIES

Alice Betrothed (coming soon)

For my dear nieces
Stacy and Lindsay Gordon

Wisconsin and London are one thing,
but please don't move to Wales.
I don't cope well in the wilderness.

ONE

Grosmont Grange, England
December 20, 1651

*L*ADY CHRYSTABEL Trevor adored Christmas.

Or at least she had until this year.

She frowned as her sap-sticky hands wove yet another wreath from the greenery she and her younger sister had collected. "Just five more days," she said, thinking of all the decorating they still had to do.

Arabel meticulously measured two loops of red ribbon. "But just four days until Christmas Eve."

"Yes, and we have to be ready by Christmas Eve." Chrystabel sighed as she eyed the enormous pile of boughs they'd cut and trimmed. "I cannot believe how long it took to make the garlands. This isn't easy alone."

"You're not alone, Chrystabel." Arabel sounded sweetly sympathetic. "I'm still here. Matthew's still here."

"Martha and Cecily aren't here." Martha and Cecily were their older sisters. "And neither is Mother." Not that Mother had helped her girls prepare for Christmas, anyway. She'd always been a rather uninvolved parent, leaving her children to be raised by nursemaids. But this was their first Christmas without her, and having her home and not participating had been better than not having her with them at all. "It makes me sad that we never see her."

"Just pretend she's dead," Arabel suggested airily.

Arabel said everything airily. Pretty, seventeen-year-old Arabel was dark-haired and dark-eyed and statuesque—like Chrystabel and the rest of the Trevors—and she was the happiest person Chrystabel knew. Nothing ruffled her. She could find the good side of anything.

Unabated cheerfulness like that set Chrystabel's teeth on edge.

"Mother is not dead," she pointed out unnecessarily. "I could forgive her if she were dead." Their father had died, after all—fighting for the king in the Civil War—and Chrystabel had never blamed *him* for leaving them. Death was sad but normal.

But there was nothing normal about being alive and not even an hour's ride away—and ignoring your own children.

Especially at Christmas.

Chrystabel set her jaw. "I will never forgive her for marrying that...*that* man."

That man was the Marquess of Bath, and he had no interest in the grown children of his second wife. The sorry and shocking thing was that Mother seemed similarly disinclined to spend time with her first family. She was too busy with her new husband and his children that she was raising. *Raising.* Even though she'd barely deigned to notice Chrystabel and her brother and three sisters—the five children she'd given birth to—all the years they were growing up.

"You cannot let Mother's selfishness ruin our Christmas," Arabel chided. "We're not children anymore. Let it go. I have. Martha and Cecily have."

"Martha and Cecily are married with children of their own. They don't need a mother anymore."

"For heaven's sake, Chrys, you're nineteen years old—you don't need a mother anymore, either." Arabel handed her a perfect red bow. "Here. Attach it, and that's one more wreath finished."

"Still twelve more to make," Chrystabel said with a sigh.

Arabel's laugh sounded suspiciously like a snort. "You're the one who insists upon decorating this entire, huge house."

Arabel was right about that—and more. Chrystabel knew she needed to dispense with the anger she felt toward their mother. It served no purpose. She would take a lesson from her less-than-ideal childhood: When she had her own family, she would do better.

Right then and there, she determined to do better.

"Look." For once, Arabel wore a frown. She motioned out the window. "Soldiers. Parliamentarian soldiers."

Hearing hoofbeats approach down Grosmont Grange's long, icy, hard-packed drive, Chrystabel dragged her thoughts from her mother to follow her sister's gaze. Sure enough, the horsemen wore breastplates over buff leather coats, with lobster-tailed pot helmets on their heads. Oliver Cromwell's Dragoons.

They couldn't be bringing good news to a Royalist family.

Since the war had ended in September, the formerly fighting Dragoons were now roaming the countryside, enforcing Cromwell's strict Puritanical laws: no music, no dancing, no theater, no sports, no swearing, no drinking, no gaming...no Christmas.

No Christmas!

"They mean to catch us preparing for Christmas!" Chrystabel ran from the chamber and down the corridor to her brother's study. "Matthew, open up!" Without waiting, she pushed open the door and burst inside. "Dragoons! Here to catch us celebrating Christmas!"

Arabel had already scooped up as much greenery as she could carry and was racing past the open door. "Where should we put it?" she called.

"Under your bed, then go back for more—we'll put it under mine!" Chrystabel turned back to Matthew. "We'll hide everything. You answer the door when they arrive."

It took three trips to and from the drawing room to hide all the Christmas evidence beneath their two beds. Once the sisters were finished, they shut the door to Chrystabel's room and plopped onto the mattress side by side, pretending to be reading books.

"Surely they won't look under our beds," Arabel whispered in her usual cheerful manner.

"We can hope not," Chrystabel muttered back.

Time passed while she listened to her own heartbeat and reread the same paragraph thirteen times.

"I don't hear anyone searching the house," Arabel said. "And they were wearing heavy boots."

Chrystabel shrugged. "As you recently pointed out, it's a big house. They'll get here."

They both jumped when a sharp knock came at the door.

Chrystabel steeled herself. "Enter if you must."

"I must," their brother said as the door swung open.

"Matthew! Are they gone?"

"They are." He suddenly looked older than his twenty-five years. His handsome face appeared ashen. For the first time, he looked like the Earl of Grosmont to her, not just her big brother who unfortunately had inherited early.

"Why did they not search my chamber?"

"They didn't search anything." He held up a letter with a big, broken red seal hanging from it. A very official-looking letter. "They brought this."

"What does it say?" Arabel breathed.

Leaning against the doorpost as though he couldn't quite hold himself up, Matthew cleared his throat and read. "'I thought fit to send this trumpet to you, to let you know that, if you please to walk away with your family and staff, and deliver your estate to such as I shall send to receive it, you shall have liberty to take one day to gather and carry off your goods, and such other necessaries as you have. You have failed to pay the fine assessed by the Committee for Compounding; if you necessitate me to bend my cannon against you, you may expect what I doubt you will not be pleased with. I await your present answer, and rest your servant, O. Cromwell.'"

"Oh, my God." Arabel's big brown eyes had never looked wider. "Did you give the soldiers your answer?"

"I had to. They wouldn't leave without it."

"And what was your answer?" Chrystabel asked impatiently. "What did you say?"

"That we'll leave, of course. Tomorrow, as he ordered. What else could I say?" Matthew straightened up. Some color had returned to his face. "The fine is a third of the value of this estate. I don't have that much money—Father spent all our savings on the war."

"The heartless bastards!" Chrystabel would be fined herself if the Dragoons heard her using that kind of language, but right now she didn't care. "How dare they!"

Matthew shrugged. "Our family dared to fight against them. Now they'll confiscate our estate for their own gain. They need funds to run the new government—if the king had won, he'd have robbed the other side just the same. We are but the spoils of war."

Matthew was a very levelheaded fellow, always good in a crisis. Unlike Chrystabel, who couldn't seem to think straight. "But what will we do? Where will we go?"

"Grosmont Castle." On his walk from the front door to her room, he'd obviously thought this through. "My seat. It's supported us ever since Father died. And it's the only place we *can* go,isn't it?" he added reasonably.

"We're to live in Wales?" Chrystabel shrieked, her volume not reasonable at all.

"My, that is far away," Arabel murmured.

"Yes, and what about all our friends?" Being a sociable sort, Chrystabel had many friends. "We won't make new ones—Wales is nothing but wilderness! And we don't even know their language! Their words have all those L's!"

"I'd wager there are no Dragoons there," Arabel pointed out, looking on the bright side as always. "We won't need to worry about Cromwell coming after *that* drafty old castle."

"We can be thankful for that," Matthew agreed. "I imagine we should instruct the servants to begin packing our things."

Chrystabel shook her head, amazed that her brother could be so calm and practical. She remained silent a moment, struggling to resign herself to this dire fate.

Wales.

Wales!

She slipped a hand into her pocket and played with the silver pendant she kept there, which always made her feel better. Father had given it to her right before he left to go fight in the war, when she'd been inconsolable. It was a family heirloom, a rendering of the Grosmont crest with its lion, passed down the generations from father to son…and now to Chrystabel. Tradition said the lion pendant ought to be Matthew's, but Chrystabel only paid heed to traditions that suited her. And losing her dearest keepsake of the man she'd loved most in all the world would not suit her one bit.

Her heart constricted at the thought of everything else she was about to lose. Her ancient tester bed, where she'd spent most every night of her nineteen years. The harpsichord her mother used to play when they had company to supper. The little rose garden her father had planted for her…

"I'm taking my roses," she said suddenly, surprising even herself.

Matthew's dark brows knitted together. "What?"

"I'm taking my roses. I need them for essential oils to make perfume, and I haven't any idea whether there will be roses in Wales at all, let alone *my* roses."

Arabel shook her head. "They're *planted*, Chrystabel. You cannot take roses."

"What did Cromwell say?" Chrystabel marched over to snatch the letter from Matthew's hand and quote from it. "'You shall have liberty to take one day to gather and carry off your goods, and such other necessaries as you have.'" She looked up. "I'm a perfumer. I consider my roses necessary."

"You cannot take them," Arabel repeated. "There's no point. They'll die."

"It's winter. They're dormant." Chrystabel hoped that meant they wouldn't die.

"You cannot take them," Arabel insisted.

"You think not?" The look Chrystabel sent her sister was a challenge. "Watch me."

TWO

Tremayne Castle
December 22

JOSEPH ASHCROFT, the Viscount Tremayne, was puttering around in his—well, he liked to call it his conservatory, even though it really wasn't one—when he heard the old wooden door rattling, making quite a racket.

A shout forced its way through the cracks. "Please, let me in!"

"You cannot go in there, Mistress," one of Tremayne's groundsmen hollered as the door rattled some more—to no avail, since it was barred from the inside. "This wing is unfinished and uninhabited. You must go around the castle and through the gatehouse."

"I cannot—it's urgent!"

"That door won't open from out here. You really must go around, Mistress...?"

"Creath Moore—my name is Creath Moore." The groundsman must have looked confused, because she added, "Creath—it rhymes with *breath*. And I must get inside *now!*"

Joseph was already unbolting the door. When he lifted the bar and pulled it open, Creath fell into his arms.

And immediately began sobbing on his shoulder.

"I've got her, thanks," Joseph told the groundsman, who was standing there looking astonished to find anyone in the roofless building.

A new hire. Otherwise he would have known that Joseph used this half-built wing of the castle for his winter gardening—and the man would also have known Creath. She lived on the nearest estate, and she and Joseph had been friends for nearly ten years, ever since his family had moved here to Tremayne to wait out the Civil War in relative safety. He and Creath had grown up together. All of the old retainers knew her.

In ten years, Joseph couldn't remember Creath ever sobbing this hard. Not even when her parents and little brother all died of smallpox last year. She wasn't a short girl, but he was tall, and she felt slight and fragile shuddering against him. He couldn't imagine what was so wrong, but his heart went out to her.

"Close the door," she managed through her sobs. "And bar it. Please."

Joseph disentangled himself from her to do that, shutting the door in the groundsman's surprised face.

"Will you be all right?" he asked Creath once they were free from prying eyes.

"Yes. No. I don't know." Choking back more tears, she staggered over to his potting bench and dropped to one of the stools he kept nearby. Her gaze darted around the huge open space to all the glassless windows, which Joseph had covered in oiled parchment that let in light but blocked any view. "Will you look outside and see if anyone is approaching?"

Joseph blinked. "You just asked me to bar the door. Now you want me to unbar it? No one is there other than the groundsman—who else would be out in this freeze? The way the wind is gusting off the icy Severn, I fear we're in for a storm—"

"I need to know if Sir Leonard followed me—just look!"

At twenty, Joseph already knew that he'd never understand females. But he could tell that this one was on the edge of hysteria.

"Very well." Hands held up in surrender, he backed away until he hit the door, then turned, opened it, and quickly shut and barred it again. "There's no one. It's so damned cold—" He broke off as he turned back to peer at her. "And yet, you wear no cloak. Did you *walk* here from Moore Manor with no cloak? Over a mile in the freezing cold?"

"There was no time to fetch a cloak. And I didn't walk here, I ran, which warmed me some." Although all four fireplaces were lit, and the oiled canvas overhead held in the heat to keep his plants alive, she shivered. "I feel cold now, though. I cannot go through with it, Joseph. I cannot marry Sir Leonard. I just cannot."

Sir Leonard Moore, the rather distant cousin who had recently inherited her father's baronetcy, expected to wed her on the second of January, the day before she turned eighteen. He coveted her hold-ings—acres of valuable land that weren't included in the baronetcy's entail, as they'd come from her mother's family and now belonged to Creath. Unfortunately for her, Cromwell had seen fit to appoint Sir Leonard her guardian, which meant she couldn't refuse to marry him. As long as she was underage, her marriage rights were his to bestow.

But up until now, she hadn't objected to the match. When Joseph had questioned her, Creath had claimed she didn't mind wedding a man more than twice her age. She'd always been destined to be a lady of the manor, and her mother had trained her well. Though she wished Moore Manor weren't Sir Leonard's manor, at least it was home. She'd told Joseph she would be content loving her children and caring for her tenants and ancestral lands. And one day, her son would be the next baronet, bringing the title back to her branch of the family where it belonged.

He'd believed her. He'd believed she'd make the best of her passionless marriage and take pleasure in the tasks expected of a lady. Because Creath was the kind of woman who would compromise her very soul in order to avoid conflict. The kind of woman who would square her shoulders, lift her chin, and get on with her life no matter what happened.

Clearly something had changed.

"What on earth happened?" Joseph reached to smooth the straight reddish-blond hairs that had escaped her usually neat bun.

Creath flinched from him, her arms wrapping around her middle. "He tried to bed me," she stated bluntly. The girl could be honest to a fault. "He said he wanted to make sure I wouldn't change my mind, make sure no other man would want me if I did change my mind." Her lower lip quivered. "If you'd seen the look in his eyes, Joseph—I believe he is insane."

"Holy Hades." Something had changed, all right: The man had proved himself an animal. "He...he didn't succeed, though?"

She shook her head, biting her lip to stop the quivering. "I begged, and then I fought, and he was hurting me. I grabbed one of Father's heavy bronze statues and brought it down on his head. He dropped like a sack of flour...and I ran."

It wrenched at his guts, watching her struggle for control. She clearly wanted to act like her normal, levelheaded self. But she didn't seem to know how.

The bastard had really shaken her. Joseph wasn't a violent man, but right then, he'd never felt more capable of murder.

"May I hide here?" she asked.

"Of course you can," he told her, though he knew that was his father's decision to make.

Joseph's title was just a courtesy title. Someday he'd be the Earl of Trentingham, but until then his father was the lord and head of the family. Still, he knew his parents would agree to give Creath safe harbor. They loved her like a daughter.

"We'll keep you safe," he promised, hoping they could. "I think we can assume Sir Leonard didn't follow you, since he would have arrived by now."

"I hope he's still knocked out," she said darkly.

"Do you think he'll guess where you've gone?"

"Maybe. I'm not sure. He doesn't know me very well." It had taken quite some time for the authorities to trace the Moore lineage back far enough to find and verify her father's heir—Sir Leonard had arrived only last month. "I'm hoping he doesn't know which neighbors are my friends. If I can hide for ten days, I'll turn eighteen, and he won't be my guardian anymore. He won't be able to make me marry him then."

"I'm not so sure, Creath. He's a Justice of the Peace." That appointment was another reward from Cromwell—Sir Leonard claimed to have fought beside him in the war. "Marriage is a civil matter now, no longer any business of God's. If a Justice of the Peace can marry others, who's to say he can't also marry himself? He just has to write your two names in his register. The old ways are gone..."

"Oh, God, they're all corrupt, aren't they?"

"Not all. But certainly some." Probably most. And he strongly suspected Sir Leonard was among the corrupt ones.

"I cannot marry him. I cannot." Creath had always been a lovely pale English beauty, but now she looked positively white. "I've seen his true colors. He came from nothing, and he's not a nice man. He's a baronet now and has a government post, a solid position in society. But he wants more. He'll always want more. He thinks marrying me will satisfy him, but it won't, because he will never be satisfied with anything. He will grow to hate me and torment me till the end of my days."

By the end of her speech, her pretty green eyes were leaking steadily.

Joseph plopped onto the stool beside her, and they both sat silent for a long time. The wind howled outside, making the canvas billow overhead. The weather was kicking up. Grasping for a solution that seemed just out of his mental reach, Joseph heaved a frustrated sigh.

"Well, there's nothing for it," he said lightly. "You'll just have to spend the rest of your days in hiding." If he couldn't solve her problems, perhaps he could at least revive her good humor. "Remember the priest hole?"

It was hidden beneath the false bottom of a wardrobe cabinet— they'd played in it as children. She gave him a wan smile. "Alas, I'm not sure I could last even one day in there, let alone the rest of my days."

"Oh, you wouldn't have that many," he quipped. "You'd die of starvation quick enough." In Queen Elizabeth's time, more than one priest had starved to death in a priest hole. The secret rooms were originally built to hide fugitive Catholics, who'd sometimes languished in them for days or weeks when the priest-hunters came around.

Creath's little smile turned lopsided. "I'd wager I'd succumb to madness first. It's pitch-black in there, and I loathe the dark."

"I'll take that wager—and see you well supplied with candles."

He thought she almost chuckled. "You're too—" Her smile faltered. He waited. "Creath?"

"I'm sorry." Her red-rimmed eyes seemed to focus on something far away. "Thanks for trying," she whispered.

They fell into another silence. The canvas continued flapping, and a few snowflakes found their way inside. Joseph rose and took his time adding another log to each of the four fires, considering all the aspects of her dreadful dilemma. Examining the problem from every angle. Wracking his brain for any possible way out.

At last, it was Creath's turn to heave a sigh. "Maybe he's not as corrupt as we fear. Maybe he'll give up once I'm eighteen."

"And if he doesn't?" he said, returning to her. "If your name ends up in his marriage register?"

"I don't know what I'd do." Her lip was trembling again, her face paler than a ghost's. "I cannot be bound to a man who tried to rape me. I...I think I'd rather not live at all."

"Don't say that!" Joseph wanted to take her in his arms, but he wasn't sure she was ready to be touched. What if he frightened her again and made everything worse?

He didn't know what to do for her, this Creath who was so unlike his Creath. The girl he'd grown up with was steady and resourceful, relentlessly good-natured, always thinking of others. There weren't a lot of people of his age and social status so far out in the countryside, but that had never mattered, because Creath was so easy to get along with. Though three years lay between them, they'd been the best of friends very nearly since the day they'd met.

He sat beside her again. There had to be an answer. He was smart. He was logical. He knew how to think things through.

And his best friend needed him.

How could he save her from that brute without hiding her in a priest hole forever?

"I'll marry you," he said quite suddenly.

"What?"

"I'll marry you. We'll go to Bristol and find a Justice of the Peace. The weather is worsening now, but we'll go as soon as it's better." Bristol was only twelve miles away—unless the weather was absolutely awful, they could get there. "We'll go well ahead of your planned wedding day for sure. Sir Leonard won't be able to force you to marry him if you're already wed to me."

She looked horrified. Not desolate like she had at the prospect of wedding Sir Leonard, but truly horrified. "I cannot marry you, Joseph!"

"Why not? It's the perfect solution." And once Joseph Ashcroft found a solution, he stuck with it...even if he found the idea a tad bit horrifying himself.

She shook her head. "It isn't the perfect solution!"

"I think it is. We won't want to wait too long—we won't want to give Sir Leonard too much time to find you, but—"

"Joseph! You're not listening! I cannot marry you. It wouldn't be fair to you. I—I love you, but not *like that*."

"Why on earth should that matter?" He pinned her with the most persuasive gaze he could muster. "You don't love Sir Leonard *like that* either. In fact, you don't love him at all. Yet until today you were prepared to marry him."

"That was different. He wasn't giving me a choice, and he wasn't foolishly sacrificing his own happiness to secure mine."

"Marrying you won't mean sacrificing my happiness," Joseph said, wondering if he was sacrificing his happiness.

But of course he wasn't. He'd thought this through, hadn't he? He always thought things through before making decisions.

It was true that he hadn't expected to marry at twenty. Hell, he hadn't expected to marry before thirty. But what did that matter?

Father didn't want to be anywhere within Cromwell's easy reach while he was in power, which was why they were here at Tremayne.

Now that the war had ended and the wrong side had won, Joseph figured he'd be stuck here the rest of his life. And the only suitable girl close to his age here was Creath, so why not marry her? He might not love her *like that*, but he liked her a lot. And it wasn't as though he would find anyone else. There was no one else to find.

"Maybe we'll fall in love *like that* after being married a while," he said, although he didn't think it likely. They'd known each other ten years already and hadn't fallen in love. But it was *possible*.

Wasn't it?

Did it matter?

He had to save Creath.

"I'm not going to fall in love with you, Joseph. Which doesn't signify, because your idea won't work." Apparently she had decided to change tacks. "I'm still seventeen. I won't be able to marry without Sir Leonard's permission while he's still my guardian."

"Most of the justices are corrupt, remember? There are at least a dozen of them in this county. And more than a few respect my father. Those who were appointed before the regicide remember when the Earl of Trentingham was a very powerful man." Though he felt a little sick to his stomach, he forced a confident smile. "I'm sure Father can direct me to a justice who will happily write our names in his register even though you're a few days shy of eighteen. I'll give him money, and he'll conveniently forget to ask your age. And it will be done. And you will be safe."

"And you will be miserable."

"I will not. You're my friend. My best friend. I've always suspected that marriage to a friend might be the best sort of marriage anyhow."

That wasn't true—he'd never suspected anything of the kind. But it sounded good, didn't it? He'd said it so earnestly that it sounded good to him.

"I don't know…" She was weakening.

"Come here." He rose and brought her up with him, moving slowly so as not to startle her. Holding her hands, he felt nothing special, nothing exciting, nothing new. Not even the spark of desire he felt with other girls, with the villagers' daughters who'd tumbled him in his youth, and the ones he'd later tumbled himself. Being near them had been thrilling. Being near Creath was...pleasant.

He was planning to marry her, but she was still just Creath Moore, his childhood friend.

He tilted her face up and pressed a chaste kiss to her lips, and still he felt nothing special.

But kissing her didn't feel bad, either. It felt nice. Comfortable. And he couldn't abandon her to her cousin Sir Leonard, a man who made her shiver with cold in a conservatory heated by four fireplaces.

She was sweet and kindhearted, and she didn't deserve such a fate. "Will you marry me, Creath?"

"I suppose so."

"Pray *try* to contain your excitement," he said with a forced laugh. "Let's go tell my parents."

THREE

December 23

HREE DAYS INTO the Trevors' journey, the weather took a turn for the worse.

Not that the weather had been pleasant to begin with. Chrystabel felt like she hadn't been warm in days, and the churned-up winter roads had made for a bumpy ride. She was convinced their carriage had managed to find every rut from Bath to Bristol.

But today's cold was something else, something malicious, with biting winds and just enough damp to make the chill penetrate down to the bone. Her fingers and toes were achingly numb, though she wore two extra pairs of stockings and kept her gloved hands bundled in her pockets. Even through leather, the lion crest pendant felt like a chip of ice in her palm. Holding it brought her little comfort today.

In short, she was thoroughly miserable. And they weren't even in Wales yet.

When she wasn't too busy wallowing, she was worrying. She worried for her roses, which had been carefully wrapped and lovingly secured in the baggage wagon, and for her Christmas decorations, hastily flung atop the load. At the last minute she'd decided Christmas was coming with them, Cromwell's laws be damned.

In two days' time, she would have her Yuletide celebration. She didn't care where. She would decorate the carriage if it came to that.

But now she worried her treasured roses and hand-trimmed boughs might not make it to Christmas Day. Could any living thing—or recently living, in the case of the boughs—survive such bitter cold and relentless jostling?

Most of all, she worried for the servants, who were bringing up the rear in two ancient carriages with no glass in the windows. Some of their retainers had chosen to stay behind in Wiltshire, but most feared being out of work in these turbulent times. Though Chrystabel and her sister had loaned them all the spare cloaks and blankets they could find, she feared the poor dears might be icicles by day's end.

If only Matthew had the funds to buy some decent, modern vehicles...

But then, if her brother had a great heap of money at his disposal, they wouldn't have lost Grosmont Grange.

"L-look," Arabel said through chattering teeth. Hugging herself tighter, she leaned toward the window. "It's s-snowing again."

Chrystabel's sigh made a little puff of fog. "We ought to stop somewhere."

"On account of this bit of fluff?" Matthew's jaw was clenched and his posture unnaturally stiff; he was far too manly to allow himself to shiver. "Regardless, there's nothing nearby—"

"Is that a c-castle?" Peering through the window, Arabel brightened. "Yes, just there off the road, p-peeking up through the woods. And there's smoke rising from its chimneys. Someone m-must be home!"

Matthew leaned to see what she was talking about. "Probably just a skeleton staff who won't want to take us in," he muttered. "And the place isn't 'just off the road,' either—it's got to be nearly a mile away."

"That's certainly closer than Wales," Chrystabel snapped, though in truth, she had no idea where they were in relation to Wales. She just knew they still had a long journey ahead of them. The ferry crossing at New Passage had been closed due to the weather, the River Severn too frozen for the ferryman to risk. Now they had to go all the way to Gloucester before they could loop around the river and head west to Grosmont Castle.

"In this weather, whoever's at that c-castle will feel obligated to take us in, even if the owners aren't p-p-present." Arabel was shivering so hard that Chrystabel suspected it was half for show.

Chrystabel nodded. "Think of our staff, Matthew. We must find them shelter. If *you'd* rather freeze to death, you're welcome to wait in the carriage."

"Oh, very well," he grumbled. "But I fear this will prove a waste of time." He knocked on the carriage roof and told the bundled-up coachman to turn off the road, trusting the rest of the train would follow. "If we have to turn back, I'm going to say 'I told you so,'" he warned afterward.

The castle turned out to be *more* than a mile off, and Chrystabel held her tongue the entire way. But her heart sank when they got close enough to see the structure was only half-built.

With its tall, decorative brickwork chimneys and other Tudor architectural touches, she'd thought the castle belonged to the previous century—but now she feared it was new and just built in that style. What if only construction workmen were there? Picturing her family's carriages turning around to head back to the main road, she felt colder than ever.

But to her very great relief, a footman greeted their arrival. Chrystabel showed remarkable restraint as the man asked their names, scurried off to "consult with milord," and reappeared to graciously welcome them all into the castle. Only then did she turn to her brother and crow, "I told you so!"

Matthew may or may not have looked daggers at her as she led the way inside. She didn't see, because she was too busy noticing the gentleman who waited in the wood-paneled entry hall.

Or rather, not just noticing. To her astonishment, she found herself *gaping*. Tall and trim, the man was young, nearly as young as she. He had deep green eyes and long, wavy jet-black hair—Cavalier hair, which meant he was Royalist, like her family.

Just occupying the same space with this stranger was having peculiar effects on her body. She didn't feel nervous, as she sometimes had around other good-looking men. Instead, she felt soft and warm both inside and out. She felt *thawed* in a way that had nothing to do with coming in out of the cold.

She couldn't not look at him. She willed him to glance her way. His gaze met hers—

—and her heart came to a stop.

It just paused, as if suspended in time for as long his eyes held hers.

A sudden truth occurred to her: *I'm going to marry this man.*

Which was ridiculous, when she thought about it. Maybe she was overtired.

Yes, she had to be overtired. The frozen, uncomfortable journey had been exhausting.

When he looked away to address her brother, the perplexing moment passed. "Welcome to Tremayne, Lord Grosmont." His voice was deep and as beautiful as the planes of his face, making Chrystabel melt a little more. "I would ask what brings you to my home, except I fear I know the answer. I hope the weather will not delay your travels long."

"My profound thanks, uh…" Matthew trailed off, apparently realizing too late that their host hadn't named himself.

Chrystabel suddenly had to know his name. "Who are you?" she blurted.

Thoughtful eyes fixed on her again, and again her heart paused. "My name is Joseph Ashcroft, my lady. The Viscount Tremayne," he added with a little formal bow she found amusing.

Or maybe it was *be*musing. She was certainly feeling bemused.

Matthew poked her in the ribs. "This is my rude sister, Lady Chrystabel Trevor. My courteous sister is Lady Arabel Trevor. And we are most grateful for your hospitality, Lord Tremayne."

The viscount flashed straight white teeth in a smile that nearly reduced her to a puddle. "The hospitality is my father's. He's regrettably detained, but he hopes you and your lovely sisters will join our family supper tonight."

Lovely! Could he have meant Chrystabel? Or was he just being polite?

"We'd be delighted," Matthew answered for all three of them.

Lord Tremayne nodded. "The dining room is rather hidden, so shall we meet here again at seven? In the meantime, our housekeeper will settle your staff and belongings, and Watkins here will show you to our guest chambers. Please make yourselves at home."

With another droll little bow, the viscount took his leave. Chrystabel stayed rooted in place until he was entirely out of sight. When she blinked herself awake, her siblings were gone.

She caught up to them on a wide flight of stone stairs, which had twisted wrought-iron balusters and a dark oak handrail. The staircase led to a long corridor that appeared to run the length of the building, torches lighting it at intervals.

Though she'd assumed a half-built castle would be unfinished inside, too, this portion was a beautiful and sumptuous home. Trailing Watkins, Chrystabel passed a costly gilt mirror and several impressive tapestries, skimming her hand along stone block walls polished to a subtle sheen.

Watkins hurried ahead to open a door on the left. "Would one of the ladies like this chamber?"

Chrystabel peeked into a spacious, splendid room. "I would love it," she said, rushing inside before her sister could claim it.

The first detail that caught her eye was a set of magnificent oriel windows. Amazingly, the glass window panes were curved. Marveling, she drifted closer and counted four banks of curved windows projecting out from the back wall, each shaped like a rounded flower petal. She'd never seen anything like them. They afforded a stunning view of the walled Tudor landscape below.

The geometric garden was lightly dusted with snow. "The grounds were designed by the young viscount," Watkins explained, "in the style of Tradescant the Elder."

Chrystabel loved flowers and knew John Tradescant had brought seeds and bulbs to England from all over the world. She found herself as entranced by Lord Tremayne's gardens as she was by the man himself. "Oh, these grounds must be enchanting in summer!" She longed to see them in full bloom.

Too bad she'd be in godforsaken Wales.

Excusing himself with a bow far more proper than his master's, Watkins ushered Arabel and Matthew back out. "My lady, I hope you'll find the next room over to your liking," Chrystabel heard as he led them down the corridor. "Lord Grosmont, you'll be installed across the way."

When she finally tore herself from the view, Chrystabel closed the room's door and then surveyed the rest of her surroundings with almost equal glee. Her bedchamber at Grosmont Grange had been nice, but not as nice as this one. It boasted a four-poster bed with red curtains and a red canopy, much like her tester bed at home, but newer and better quality. A carved stone fireplace blazed merrily on one wall, and a red Oriental carpet cushioned the floor beneath her feet. Besides the bed, she had a carved wardrobe cabinet and a lovely dressing table with another costly mirror. In the cozy rounded space created by the oriel windows sat an inlaid hexagonal table with two well-stuffed chairs.

She was already regaining the feeling in her fingers and toes, and with any luck, she'd get to stay warm and snug in this gorgeous room through Christmas. The impending misery of Wales felt like a distant bad dream. Tremayne seemed no place for such unpleasant thoughts.

Remembering she was overtired, she crawled into the big bed and burrowed beneath the plush counterpane. While waiting to doze off, she pictured Lord Tremayne designing an exquisite new garden. A rose garden. For her.

Goodness, but he looked darling when he was concentrating.

In the summertime, the rose garden he'd planted for her bloomed. The colors were spectacular, the fragrances breathtaking. And she was here to enjoy it all. She lived here, at splendid Tremayne. And she lived here because—

A knock startled her awake.

Chrystabel scrambled out of bed to open her door. "Is it seven o'clock already?" she asked Arabel, patting her hair back into its austere knot.

"It will be in five minutes. Matthew went on ahead, and he said we're to meet him *on time*."

Matthew was very punctual and well-mannered and nauseatingly polite out in company. Quite different from the real Matthew that Chrystabel saw at home.

She looked Arabel up and down. "Shouldn't we change for supper?"

Arabel shrugged. "What would we change into?"

"Something more elegant," Chrystabel said, though *something more tempting* was what she meant. Her thoughts had returned to the handsome viscount.

Thanks to her nap, she was no longer overtired—and she still wanted to marry him.

Unfortunately, she feared her current attire might hamper her chances. Cromwell had forbidden bright or immodest clothing, so the gowns she wore in public were of plain fabrics in tedious browns and grays. Each one had a vast white collar that tied at the throat, concealing everything that made a female look feminine. She looked down at herself in dismay. "This will never do."

"It will have to, at least for tonight." Arabel took her arm. "They haven't brought our trunks up yet."

With a sigh of resignation, Chrystabel let her sister march her down to supper. Oh, how she longed for the fine pre-Cromwell gowns hidden in the bottom of her trunk. "Do you miss silk, Arabel? I miss silk. And damask. And embroidery and lace. I could go on all day..."

"Please don't," Arabel said good-naturedly. "You'd make us late for supper. Then Matthew would be angry, our hosts would be insulted, and we'd *still* be stuck wearing hideous brown sacks."

Chrystabel giggled. "What about velvet? Mmm, wouldn't fur-lined velvet be ever so snug on an evening like this?"

Arabel put a finger to her lips. "You forget we're in a stranger's home. Tremayne folk might frown on such talk."

"They'd better not frown at me," Chrystabel grumbled. "It's Yuletide, and just as soon as my trunk arrives I'll wear red and green whether they like it or not."

"Suit yourself." Arabel shook her head. "But we haven't seen how the lady of the house dresses yet, and I, for one, would rather look dreadful inside a warm castle than ravishing tossed out into the snow."

As usual, Arabel was right. Sometimes Chrystabel thought Arabel should be the older sister. Perhaps they'd been accidentally born in the wrong order.

Chrystabel cast about for a safe subject. "How is your chamber?"

"Marvelous. It's done up all in yellow with a very pretty four-poster bed. And best of all, it's *warm*." Arabel was easy to please. "I hope the storm doesn't break tomorrow."

"You'd like to stay longer?"

Arabel grinned. "I'd like to stay forever."

"Me, too." When they passed the fancy mirror Chrystabel had noticed earlier, she was careful to avoid her reflection. It would only upset her. "I think I shall marry the viscount."

That startled a laugh out of her sister. "Don't be a goose."

"Who's being a goose?" Chrystabel lifted her skirts to descend the staircase. "I'm perfectly serious."

"No, you're not. You don't know anything about him." Arabel gave her a sidelong glance. "Except that he's handsome and doesn't live in Wales."

For once, her younger sister was wrong. "I'm not wedding him to avoid Wales. I'm wedding him because I love him."

Now Arabel rolled her eyes. "You cannot be in love with him. You haven't even had a proper conversation with him yet."

"'Who ever loved that loved not at first sight?'" Chrystabel quoted triumphantly. "It seems Shakespeare would beg to differ."

Since Arabel was the academic of the family—she'd read nearly every book in the Grange's library—Chrystabel could rarely best her with scholarship. She relished every opportunity.

"*As You Like It* is fiction, not philosophy," her sister pointed out. "And incidentally, Shakespeare didn't even write that line. He was referencing a poem by Christopher Marlowe."

Hmmph. So much for besting Arabel.

"And there's no such thing as love at first sight, Chrys. That only happens in plays and poems."

Yesterday, Chrystabel would have agreed with that sentiment. But today she knew differently.

"What a sad, unromantic soul you are, dear sister." She patted Arabel on the shoulder. "Since it's happened to me, I suppose I'll have to prove you wrong."

FOUR

*W*HEN LORD TREMAYNE walked the Trevors into the dining room, his parents were already at the table. While Chrystabel and her siblings took their seats, the young viscount introduced them—which happily provided enough of a distraction to allow Chrystabel to maneuver herself into a seat beside him.

Lord Trentingham looked like an older version of his son, and Chrystabel was pleased to see that her future husband would remain attractive into his older years. Lady Trentingham was petite, with gleaming brown hair and her son's thoughtful green eyes. To Chrystabel's delight, she wore a lovely hyacinth-blue gown that revealed a fair expanse of skin. Right then and there, Chrystabel decided she'd be donning one of her own pretty gowns tomorrow. The red brocade, perhaps.

She couldn't wait for Lord Tremayne to see her in it.

While inquiries were being made—and condolences offered—on the direction and purpose of the Trevors' journey, another guest entered and headed toward Chrystabel. Then she paused in apparent confusion before making her way to the last remaining empty chair, on the other side of the table.

She was a fetching young woman in a modest tawny frock. "I'd be pleased for you to meet our dear friend, Mistress Creath Moore," Lady Trentingham said by way of introduction.

Seated directly across from Chrystabel, Matthew blinked. "Pray pardon, could you repeat that name?"

"Creath. It rhymes with *breath*," the young woman said with a broad smile in his direction. She was fair and looked to be about Arabel's age. "It's a family name," she added, looking pleased about that.

When the viscount leaned closer, Chrystabel caught a whiff of his scent. Rich soil, fresh greenery, and spicy wood smoke—with a hint of something mouthwatering and male underneath.

"Creath is recently orphaned," he whispered, "so bearing a family name brings her comfort, even if it is unusual."

His warm words tickled her ear. She could barely suppress a shiver. What was that delicious fragrance? She'd never smelled anything like it, in her perfumery or out.

Whatever it was, she wanted to bottle it.

And her heart was pounding madly. Why on earth did Arabel think a 'proper conversation' was a prerequisite to falling in love? The way Chrystabel felt had nothing to do with talking.

Oh, yes, she was going to marry this man. But she would have to be patient and give him time to catch up. Silly as it seemed—given the inevitability of the outcome—she'd have to work on making the viscount love her in return. Men could be blasted dim creatures when it came to this sort of thing.

No matter, she could wait. They had years and years of romantic bliss ahead of them, after all. She was a reasonable woman. She could accept that he might not fall in love with her tonight.

Tomorrow would suit her just as well.

It seemed she was becoming her own matchmaker. Now that it occurred to her, she rather thought she'd be a natural. Already, instinctively, she knew where to begin: getting Lord Tremayne to touch her.

She liked this plan. She liked it so much, her skin tingled all over. Her body felt acutely aware of the heat emanating from his. Something in her craved that heat, although she was thoroughly thawed-out now and the dining room was at a perfectly agreeable temperature.

Like everything else in this castle, the dining room was impressive. The gate-leg table they were seated at had all its leaves folded away and looked dwarfed in the big chamber. The room had dark-paneled walls, an embellished stone fireplace, pleasing paintings and tapestries, and an elaborately carved wooden minstrel's gallery at one end.

But she couldn't help noticing that something was missing.

"You've no Christmas decorations," she said to no one in particular, while two footmen set out an array of steaming dishes. "Are you not celebrating?"

"Of course we're not celebrating." Judging by the young viscount's expression, he was wondering if she were daft. "It's illegal. Meaning that would be a *crime*."

Chrystabel unleashed her silvery laugh. "Indeed, Lord Tremayne." Oh, he was too darling. "But who would catch you celebrating all the way out here?"

He raised a brow. "Out here?"

Her expansive gesture was meant to encompass the many miles between here and civilization. "Out here in the wilderness."

Tremayne wasn't quite as much in the wilderness as Wales, but it was close. The castle sat beside the River Severn, and Wales was just across it.

A corner of his mouth twitched. "We have Justices of the Peace here, as elsewhere. And surely you know that Cromwell's Roundhead spies abound." His eyes held hers for what felt like a long time, though it couldn't have been more than a few seconds. "And please, call me Joseph. We don't stand on ceremony out here in the wilderness."

Arabel and Creath let out little gasps at that impertinent request, while Joseph's parents wore matching incredulous expressions. Even the viscount seemed surprised by his own audacity.

But even though she suspected he'd said "out here in the wilderness" to poke fun at her, Chrystabel only smiled. She was liking her future husband better and better. "Then you must call me Chrystabel."

"And you can call me Creath," Creath announced, apparently loath to be excluded. Unless...had her remark been directed at Matthew? Her gaze appeared to be fastened on his. "It rhymes with *breath*," she reminded him.

Now Matthew looked incredulous.

"Wine, Lord Grosmont? My ladies?" Lord Trentingham motioned to an etched glass decanter. "It's Tremayne's own vintage," he added with a touch of pride.

"Yes, please," Matthew answered for all three of them, tearing his gaze from Creath's to nod to the earl. "And our thanks."

Chrystabel watched a footman pour the pale amber liquid. "You make wine here?" she asked, anticipating her first taste. Since the Roundheads had banned liquor, wine had become a luxury.

"You passed the vines on your way in," Lady Trentingham said. "Of course, they're dormant now, but we had a nice harvest this year. Enough for our needs and more."

"A vineyard where everyone can see it?" Chrystabel darted Joseph a look of triumph. "How fortunate that you've managed to continue the enterprise without incurring the wrath of Cromwell's spies."

Beside her, Joseph couldn't quite suppress a chuckle. "Growing grapes is not illegal."

It was her turn to raise a brow. "And what you do with the grapes...?"

"Is well hidden within the castle walls." Saluting her with his goblet, he drank.

"Wreaths and garlands would stay hidden within the castle walls as well." Chrystabel sipped the Tremayne wine. It was light, refreshing, and a little sweet, similar to Rhenish. She liked it. And it seemed to make her bold. "My sisters and I have made Christmas trimmings together every year since I can remember. It was our father's favorite holiday. During the war, he so loved coming home to see Grosmont Grange all done up in greenery and red ribbon, with all of us dressed to match. He said it reminded him what the Royalists were fighting for."

Sometimes Chrystabel was almost glad Father hadn't lived to see the outcome of the war. He would have chafed at the dull, colorless existence prescribed by the Commonwealth government. Even more than she did, he would have hated seeing beauty and joy constrained.

"What a lovely tradition," Lady Trentingham said, sounding genuine.

Chrystabel nodded. "Arabel and I were on our own with the trimmings this year, but we did our best to keep our tradition alive."

Even after Martha and Cecily had married and moved away, they'd always come home for the Yuletide season—until this year. Reluctant to incur the new regime's displeasure, the two eldest Trevor siblings and their families had kept their distance.

"I'm sure your decorations were magnificent." Lady Trentingham's smile was wistful. "It's a shame nobody will get to enjoy them."

The sisters shared a look. "Actually..." Arabel began, then bit her lip.

"We brought them with us," Chrystabel blurted.

Joseph's expression turned wary. "Oh?"

Ignoring him, she carried on addressing the countess, trying not to sound too eager. "This storm doesn't seem to be letting up," she began. As if to underscore her point, a mighty gust of wind rattled the leaded windows.

"We're in the midst of a dreadful freeze," Lady Trentingham said. "Even if it clears, you ought to stay a few more days."

Matthew nearly spit out a mouthful of wine.

"Don't you agree, dear?" the countess asked her husband.

Lord Trentingham shrugged. "*I* wouldn't travel in this weather, but if our guests want—"

"My thoughts exactly," his wife interrupted, then looked to the Trevor siblings. "You'll stay through Christmas Day, at least?"

"It would be our pleasure," Chrystabel rushed to say, thinking Matthew wasn't the only one who could answer for all of three of them. Though he'd doubtless avenge himself later, he was far too polite to contradict her in front of their hosts.

The countess nodded with satisfaction. "It's settled, then."

"And I know just how to express our gratitude," Chrystabel said. "With your permission, my lady, Arabel and I would be delighted to make you a gift of our Christmas decorations."

"Absolutely not," Lord Trentingham protested. "It's far too risky."

Chrystabel wasn't giving up. "Surely a few garlands carry no more risk than a winemaking operation—my lord," she added deferentially.

"The wine is different." Chrystabel could see why he'd want to think that: The earl was on his second glass already. "It stays hidden in the cellars. Your garlands would festoon the whole place. Anyone entering the castle could see."

"But surely no one can really threaten your family." Chrystabel watched Lord Trentingham exchange a look with his wife. "Only the House of Lords can convict a peer, and the House of Lords has been abolished."

The man shook his head. "Everything's changed. The old king is dead, and the new king is exiled. The war is over. We Royalists lost. We don't have the power we once did."

"But you're an earl."

"I'm an earl, too," Matthew unhelpfully pointed out, "and Cromwell just confiscated my home. There's no telling what will happen going forward. It would behoove us all to be careful."

Chrystabel scowled at her brother. He'd never raised these concerns before, not even when they'd been roaming the countryside with their Yuletide greenery peeking out from beneath their baggage wagon's tarpaulins. It seemed Matthew had chosen the manner of his retribution.

"There will be no Christmas celebration," Lord Trentingham declared. "Not in this house."

And that was that, Chrystabel supposed. For now. And at least they'd secured an invitation to stay a few more days.

Which should give her plenty of time to make Joseph fall in love with her.

As the next course was served, scents of roasted chicken made Chrystabel's mouth water. Having dined at inns for the length of their journey, she was grateful for the excellent meal. But when a footman offered her a dish of creamed spinach, she took just a dollop, wanting to look dainty and feminine in front of the viscount.

How could she get him to touch her?

Lady Trentingham served herself a far more generous helping of creamed spinach. "Do you enjoy any pastimes, Lady Arabel?"

"I like to read. To study, really." Arabel waved the footman on; she'd never cared for spinach. "I enjoy learning new things."

Creath likewise refused the spinach. "I enjoy reading, too." She would make a nice friend for Arabel, Chrystabel thought. The two were just the same age, and they both liked to read and disliked spinach.

"*Enjoy reading* strikes me as rather an understatement," Joseph said, bestowing a fond smile on Creath. "If I leave you alone for two minutes, I always come back to find you with your nose buried in a book."

Chrystabel wanted him to smile at *her*, not Creath. "Perfuming is my pastime," she volunteered. "Making and mixing scents, mostly from flowers and other plants. I noticed you have a wonderful Tudor garden here at Tremayne."

"That's my son's garden," Lord Trentingham told her proudly.

She'd known that, of course, but she turned to his son with feigned surprise. "How extraordinary! I've never met a viscount who gardens."

Joseph shrugged. "It's something I've always enjoyed."

"You've a true talent," she told him sincerely. "Even with the snow cover, I could tell your garden is exquisite."

He blushed faintly. "You're far too kind. It's not much to look at, really, this time of year."

"You must long for the summertime," she said, thinking of her dream.

"I prefer summer," he allowed, "but I garden in the winter, too. Indoors, in an unfinished wing of the castle. I call it my conservatory."

"An indoor garden? That's fascinating." She saw an opportunity to get him alone. "Will you show me?"

"Perhaps tomorrow, when it will be light," Lady Trentingham suggested. "He can give you and your sister a tour."

Oh, bother. Now Chrystabel would have to find an excuse to leave Arabel behind. *And* she'd have to wait until tomorrow.

She didn't want to wait that long for Joseph to touch her. She wanted it to happen tonight. It seemed very important—altogether necessary—that he touch her tonight.

She pondered that through the third course, while conversation rattled around her. Meaningless conversation. Conversation that had nothing to do with getting Joseph to touch her or fall in love with her, which meant she wasn't interested.

The fourth course was sweets. When a footman set a dish of trifle in front of her, she took a recess from pondering to savor the sugar and cream dancing on her tongue. And that gave her an idea. "Do you like to dance, Lady Trentingham?"

"I adore dancing." Joseph's mother dipped her spoon into her own trifle and sighed. "It's been ages since I danced."

Chrystabel smiled. "Should you like to dance tonight?"

"For pity's sake," Joseph burst out on a laugh, "are you a secret Roundhead attempting to entrap us?" Though she could tell he accused her in jest, the charge still stung a bit—her father had died fighting the Roundheads, after all. "Perhaps it would help if we list *every* way in which we should *not* like to break the law. No, we don't wish to attend the theater. No, we don't wish to play dice. No, we don't wish to take up highway robbery—"

"Joseph, dear, I think you've made your point," Lady Trentingham said dryly.

Falling silent, the viscount discovered a renewed interest in his trifle. He frowned in what looked like consternation, as if unsure what had come over him.

Chrystabel rather suspected it was herself.

"As it happens," the countess said conversationally," I rather *should* like to dance tonight. And before you argue, dear," she added to her husband, "this isn't like the Christmas trimmings. Should a stranger knock on the door, we can simply stop dancing, and no one will be the wiser."

Lord Trentingham grunted.

"It doesn't signify," Joseph said, "since we have no musical instruments in the house."

Chrystabel smiled sweetly. "Because music is against the law?"

He looked like he wanted to laugh. "Yes, because music is against the law. We cannot make music, hence we cannot dance." He shrugged.

"Oh, yes, we can." Chrystabel's smile stretched wider. "We've a viol and a recorder in our wagon, and willing musicians among our servants."

"Wonderful!" When Lady Trentingham's face lit up, Chrystabel realized she was very pretty for a woman her age. "It's settled, then."

The countess seemed to employ that phrase often—and to great effect. Both her husband and son appeared resigned to their fate.

I could learn much from her, Chrystabel thought.

"It's too risky," Lord Trentingham protested again, but not as though he expected anyone to listen.

"Oh, Henry," his wife admonished him, "don't be such an old fust-cudgel."

FIVE

*W*HEN THEY'D SCRAPED up every morsel of the excellent trifle and emptied the last decanter of wine, Joseph's mother announced it was time to dance. Father offered another feeble protest, but all Mother had to do was place a hand on his arm and say, "Please, dear," very winsomely while batting her eyelashes. And he gave in.

Watching the exchange, Joseph promised himself he'd never let Creath manipulate him so easily.

Not that he'd have to worry about that. His intended was the most agreeable, sweet-tempered creature on earth. She'd never employ feminine wiles to get her own way; it wouldn't even occur to her. Nor would it enter her head to make a fuss over such a frivolous matter as dancing.

Why Joseph's mother had been suddenly gripped by the need to dance was a mystery to him. Normally, Mother was a perfectly sensible woman. He couldn't imagine what had got into her.

Well, actually, he did have one idea of what—or rather, *who*—might be the cause. One who seemed rather prone to impulsive and irresponsible whims. One who exhibited little regard for propriety, and even less for the rule of law. One who, by all appearances, was here for the express purpose of getting on his nerves.

One Lady Chrystabel Trevor.

When supper first began, he'd watched her and he'd wondered. What was it about this young woman that he found so bothersome? She was a woman, after all—even hidden inside that dowdy nun's habit of a gown, she was quite unmistakably a woman. And Joseph *liked* women. He'd never met a beautiful young woman he didn't like. So why couldn't he get along with this one? It seemed every word she'd uttered was calculated to raise his hackles.

That had been irritating enough. But then she'd gone into raptures over his gardens, permanently endearing herself to him. He'd been touched—and baffled—by Chrystabel's enthusiasm. Even Creath, his oldest and dearest friend, could muster only polite praise on the subject of his gardens. Affectionate admiration, perhaps, if she were feeling generous. Gardening was the sort of pastime that elicited genuine enthusiasm only from one's parents.

And now Chrystabel.

So here he was, paradoxically endeared to someone he couldn't stand. She was the most puzzling woman he'd ever met.

"Oh, my heavens," the puzzle breathed as they stepped into the great room, "this chamber is massive."

"I believe it was used for large banquets in the last century," Mother told her.

"I've never seen such an enormous fireplace in my life. My whole family could sit inside and play Pope July!"

Mother laughed. "I wouldn't recommend it."

Having lived here for nearly ten years, Joseph never paid much notice to the great room himself. But he could see why an outsider might find this chamber particularly awe-inspiring. It had dark Tudor paneling, gilded family crests, two intimate oriel window niche seating areas, and an abundance of plush, richly upholstered furnishings—but not so much that it filled the whole space, for that would be well-nigh impossible.

"Let's push all the furniture out of the way," Chrystabel suggested.

The men jumped to do her bidding, creating a large open expanse in the center that was perfect for dancing. Chrystabel certainly knew how to command a room. Joseph wasn't sure whether he found that impressive or frightening.

Meanwhile, a footman had returned with the instruments and musicians, two spirited youths who looked so alike, they had to be brothers. "What dance shall we perform?" Mother asked while the boys readied themselves.

"We're an uneven number," Chrystabel pointed out, "one more lady than we have gentlemen."

Lady Arabel bounced on her toes. "But all the country dances are done in pairs."

"Oh, yes, that's a shame," Chrystabel said cheerfully, as though it weren't a shame at all. "And the pavane is for pairs, too. It seems the volta is our only choice."

Father gasped, then coughed. "The volta?" he choked out.

"It will suit our situation perfectly." Her honeyed smile struck Joseph as a bit too innocent. "For the galliard portion, it shan't matter if there's a spare. For the measures done with a partner, the ladies can take turns pairing with the gentlemen, and the extra lady can just twirl in place."

"But the volta is scandalous." His coughing fit under control, Father braced his hands on his hips. "It's much too intimate for a family party."

Mother made an impatient noise. "Queen Elizabeth and Queen Henrietta Maria both enjoyed the volta. It's a good Royalist dance."

"It's settled, then." Chrystabel clapped her hands. "Music, please!"

Joseph couldn't believe his ears. It was settled? Just because Chrystabel had said so? Not even here a full day, the interfering chit apparently thought herself lord of the manor—*and no one was objecting.* When the musicians raised their instruments, even Joseph moved toward the center of the room. And before he knew what was happening, he found himself beginning the galliard, a series of small leaps, jumps, and hops that could be performed without a partner.

When the beat changed to signal the partner portion of the dance, he made sure to pair up with Creath first, as was only proper. Right palm to right palm, they circled each other.

"Are you enjoying yourself?" he asked.

"As much as possible, I suppose." They switched to go the other direction, touching left palms this time. "Under the circumstances."

They didn't discuss the circumstances—not there in that room. He, Creath, and his parents had all agreed the betrothal should be kept secret from their guests, as they didn't want to risk word reaching Sir Leonard. What the Trevors didn't know, they couldn't spread to others after leaving Tremayne.

As the dance dictated, Joseph pulled Creath close, lifted her, and twirled her around. This was the part of the volta that his father found scandalous. Each of the three times he did this, Creath's exhilarated giggles escalated, making him smile. He was growing accustomed to the idea of marrying her.

Sort of.

They parted ways for another set of the energetic galliard steps. When the music changed again, he found himself paired with Chrystabel.

"Your father is very conservative," she said without preamble, raising her arm. Their hands came together palm-to-palm.

Touching Chrystabel felt so different from touching Creath that he was momentarily struck dumb. But he recovered his composure quickly as they began circling each other. "My father is indeed conservative. In fact, that's why we live so far out here *in the wilderness*. Father and Grandfather thought it safest to avoid Cromwell's notice during the war, thus they took us as far from the fighting as possible."

Her eyes flickered. "He didn't fight? My brother and father both fought in the war. Father died defending the king."

Joseph's memory flashed to when he'd accused her of being a secret Roundhead at supper. He felt immediately awful for teasing her. But he refused to feel ashamed for the difficult choices his family had made.

"My grandfather wasn't willing to risk his heir—or his grandchildren, for that matter. And after he passed, the earldom's well-being rested on my father remaining alive, at least until I was grown enough to take over if the need arose."

She leveled him her with her dark, wide-set gaze. "Meaning you placed the earldom ahead of the country."

He didn't like how that *you* made him a culprit. For pity's sake, he'd been a mere boy when they'd come to Tremayne.

But then he remembered *no one* was a culprit, because the Ashcrofts had done nothing wrong. How did she keep twisting him around in this manner?

"I suppose yours is one interpretation," he retorted as they reversed direction. "Mine might be that while other Royalists were busy killing people, we were protecting people instead. Not only our family, but the hundreds of others who depend on our lands and resources to survive."

"You think Grosmont has no dependents?" Her breath was coming faster, from annoyance or exercise or something else, he knew not. "We care about our people, too, but we made sacrifices for our king."

He shrugged. "And we chose not to make sacrifices for a hopeless cause."

Her mouth fell open in a little O that said more than words how astonished she was that any Royalist would call the monarchy a hopeless cause.

As he pulled her close for the first lift, his heart pounded in his ears—from exertion, he was sure. His hands encircled her curving waist, feeling the stiff fabric warmed by her skin. When he raised her aloft and twirled, her big white collar fluttered in his face.

He felt the oddest urge to rip the damn thing off her.

Following the third lift, it was a relief to part ways. Though the fire in the big hearth was down to embers, he was feeling overheated. His feet taking up the galliard, he wondered if he'd drunk too much wine. Or was it the stress of his impending marriage? Something must be affecting him, because he'd never acted so quarrelsome in his life, much less been afflicted with any violent, inexplicable urges.

The Ashcroft family motto was *Interroga Conformationem*, which was Latin for "Question Convention." Joseph had often thought it an unfitting motto for his family—and wondered when it might have fit and what had happened to them since. For these days, in most things, the Ashcrofts were very conventional indeed.

In contrast, he had never met a woman who questioned convention as much as Chrystabel did.

His next partner was his mother. "Lady Chrystabel is delightful, don't you think?" Mother said as they circled together.

"Delightful?"

Mother's carefully dressed curls bounced with her nod. "She's so honest and refreshing."

"Those aren't the words I would have chosen," he quipped.

"Oh?" When Mother smiled, he noticed she wasn't a bit out of breath. For that matter, neither was he, and he no longer felt over-warm, either. "Which words come to mind?"

"Impulsive," was his first choice. They changed direction. "Inter-fering. Irresponsible."

"That's a lot of *i* words," Mother said with a rare sparkle in her eye. "Have you any more?"

"Naturally." He grinned, enjoying this playful side of her. "Irritat-ing, irrational, impertinent—"

"Irresistible?" she suggested slyly.

Joseph's mouth gaped open. "Pray pardon?" Why on earth would she say such a thing?

"I saw you looking at her while the two of you danced."

"I was *not* looking at her! I happen to find her insufferable." Blast, another *i* word. It seemed he couldn't stop. "Besides which, in case you've forgotten, I'm betrothed!"

"Hush!" Mother glanced around and dropped her voice. "Our guests might overhear."

He hushed, since it was time to lift and and twirl her, anyway, which made it difficult for him to speak.

But *she* went right on ahead. "There's a lesson to be learned from this: Mere promises cannot stop one from appreciating beauty or charm when one sees it. I've been a content wife for twenty-five years, yet still I'm not immune to the charms of other men. If contentment is enough, choose the woman who will always remain by your side. But if it's happiness you seek, choose the woman who will always recapture your attention."

Now he feared his eyes were gaping—never mind that that was physically impossible. Never in his life had he heard his mother speak this way. Evidently she fit their family motto better than he'd thought. Question Convention, indeed.

After their last twirl, she detained him with a hand on his arm. "I like Lady Chrystabel. She's a pretty thing, and she makes me laugh. We haven't had a lot of laughter in this house since your sisters left." Joseph had three sisters who had all married well, thanks to the generous dowries his father had provided. He wondered if they really knew their mother. "I used to think you and your father were much alike, my dear boy. But now I see you've got more of me than I realized." And with a wink, she danced off.

Joseph performed the next galliard in a daze. He couldn't even begin turning over her surprising advice. *His mother had winked at him.*

When he found himself partnered with Lady Arabel, he managed to recover his wits. He cast about for a neutral topic of conversation. "Are you looking forward to living in Wales, Lady Arabel?"

"I'm trying to view it as an adventure." She danced in a jaunty, light-footed way that matched her cheerful nature. "I just wish I knew some Welsh."

"My father knows Welsh." He felt absurdly relieved to engage in simple, polite chitchat. "Father knows lots of languages, actually."

"Are languages his pastime?" Lady Arabel asked, as though she were really curious.

Joseph chuckled, remembering the discussion at supper. "I would say so. Shall I ask him if he might teach you a few words of Welsh?"

She squealed when he lifted her and twirled. "Oh, that would be marvelous!"

Marvelous words from a marvelous girl. For the first time this evening, he felt normal and like himself. Lady Arabel made him smile, while her sister made him...feel hot.

On a cold, snowy evening, Chrystabel Trevor made him feel hot.

It was an odd feeling he'd never experienced before, and he didn't like it one bit, he decided while performing the next set of galliard steps. It wasn't comfortable at all.

He was paired again with Creath when Watkins arrived in the great room's main doorway and cleared his throat. "Sir Leonard is approaching, my lord!" he called over the music.

SIX

*C*HRYSTABEL WATCHED Creath head for the far door at a run, dodging the jumble of pushed-aside furniture as she went.

"Keep dancing!" Lord Trentingham commanded. "Lady Arabel, take Creath's place."

Chrystabel obeyed, and so did everyone else. Arabel stepped in as Joseph's partner. Lord Trentingham was dancing with his wife, and Chrystabel was paired with Matthew. She couldn't imagine what was happening, but she kept dancing, sensing it was best not to ask.

When the set finished, Lady Trentingham signaled the musicians to skip the galliard and play them through the turns once again. Chrystabel was still circling with her brother when Watkins returned and ushered a stranger into the room.

Tall with a raw-boned build and blunt blond hair, the man was in his middle years. Though his clean-shaven features seethed with anger, his blue eyes were colder than hoarfrost. *"What is the meaning of this?"* he bellowed.

The dancers halted as the music died away. Exchanging a frightened look with her sister, Chrystabel was grateful to see Joseph placing himself between Arabel and the stranger.

"I could have you all arrested for dancing!" the man roared into the sudden silence. Then, appearing to get himself somewhat under control, he lowered his voice to a menacing growl. "And don't think I won't if I find out she's here."

Lord Trentingham furrowed his brow. "Are you searching for someone, your worship?"

Your worship? Evidently the wilderness did have Justices of the Peace—and this vile man was one of them. No wonder Tremayne folk were reluctant to break the law. Chrystabel wouldn't want to get on this brute's bad side, either.

"You know who I'm searching for." The justice's lips twisted in a sneer—an oft-used expression, judging from the deep lines around his mouth. "My *dearest* cousin and betrothed, Mistress Creath Moore."

"Good heavens, is the girl missing?" Lady Trentingham made a convincing concerned neighbor. "How long has she been gone?"

"A night and a day." The justice advanced several threatening paces toward her. "But I've an inkling you already knew that, my lady."

The earl put a protective arm around his wife. "We haven't seen the girl, Sir Leonard," he said in a tone of warning.

Chrystabel was surprised when the taller man stopped in his tracks. Then she remembered Lord Trentingham was a peer, while the justice was apparently a mere knight or baronet. He might have the advantage in malice and government authority, but the earl was a powerful man, and by no means the weaker opponent.

But Sir Leonard wasn't backing down. An inflamed red lump on his head, just visible beneath his thinning hair, seemed to pulse with anger. "I've searched all the other nearby estates and found no trace of her," he snarled.

He'd saved Tremayne for last, Chrystabel noted. Further proof he was afraid of the earl.

"You're welcome to search our grounds," Lady Trentingham put in, "though the cold—"

"What I *did* find," he interrupted rudely, "was a universal consensus among our neighbors that my cousin was most likely to be found with the Ashcrofts."

Joseph stepped forward, his right hand moving to his hip—where a sword hilt would have rested had he been formally attired. "We already told you she's not here," he snapped.

Lady Trentingham held out a restraining arm. "Please excuse my son, your worship. He means no disrespect. But I'm afraid he's right. Mistress Moore is not with us. If she were, she would have prevented us from dancing."

Sir Leonard barked a laugh. "Don't trifle with me, my lady. I have no illusions regarding my bride's proclivities. Her intimates are all depraved Cavaliers, every last one of you. If you called on her to dance, she wouldn't bat an eyelash."

"You mistake my meaning, your worship." Astoundingly, the countess maintained her composure in the face of his insults. "I was merely referring to the balance of the genders. If Mistress Moore were present, we would have one too many ladies."

Sir Leonard made a show of balking, but Chrystabel could see him mentally counting heads. "Very well," he said at last. "I shall expand my search further afield. But if I learn you're withholding information…"

"We shall, of course, notify you the instant we hear of her whereabouts," Lord Trentingham held out his hand. "We're as worried about her as you are."

Chrystabel had a hard time believing the brute ever worried about anyone besides himself. He appeared to lack the required muscles.

With another of his frequent sneers, Sir Leonard refused the offered hand. "Let me be clear, Trentingham. If it emerges that you are *in any way* hindering my search, you and your family will suffer dire consequences. Full cooperation will be rewarded. Anything less will be punished—severely."

"I understand, your worship." The earl gave a curt nod.

"Also understand that you are still under suspicion. Would that I could make a thorough search of your home tonight, but I'm afraid I haven't the necessary…expertise."

Chrystabel wondered what he meant by that. What special knowledge could be required for searching a home?

The earl cleared his throat. "Begging your pardon, Sir Leonard, but I must remind you that you are on my property. I have not gone so far as to bar you from paying a social call"—Chrystabel nearly burst out laughing at the absurdity of labeling this 'a social call'—"but such will be the extent of my hospitality."

"As I expected." The justice waved a hand, as if he weren't bothered. In fact, Chrystabel could have sworn she saw a triumphant gleam in his eye. "I've already sent for a force to help me scour the countryside. Shall twenty armed men be sufficient to compel entry?"

Matthew's hand tightened around Chrystabel's—she hadn't even realized he'd been holding it. Joseph grunted, Lady Trentingham gasped, and Lord Trentingham looked like he was about to be sick.

And Sir Leonard smirked. "Parliament's justice will not be subverted. I shall have my men on Saturday, and if my bride hasn't yet returned, I'll be bringing them here first. Good evening."

With that, he turned on a heel and left.

SEVEN

HE MOMENT THE heavy front door thudded to a close behind the Justice of the Peace, everyone in the great room audibly released their breaths.

"I'll get her," Joseph said.

He strode toward the same doorway Creath had disappeared through. Inexorably curious, Chrystabel trailed him. To her great surprise, no one tried to stop her. She assumed they were too stunned by the news of an imminent attack on the castle to bother themselves over a girl's inappropriate prowling.

But after passing through a drawing room and into another corridor, she looked back and realized everyone else was coming along, too.

They all turned a corner to find a maidservant standing there—standing guard, it would appear. She acknowledged Joseph with a nod, then pulled a crowbar out of a nearby cupboard and handed it to him.

Chrystabel followed Joseph into a bedchamber and across it, where he unlatched the double doors of a wardrobe cabinet that looked exceedingly large and heavy. Fitting the crowbar into one end of the base, he used it to pry up the bottom. The panel of wood came loose, revealing an opening in the floor that had been hidden.

Chrystabel gasped when she saw Creath ascending what looked to be a very steep staircase that led down into a dark space below.

"Watch out for the third step," Joseph said, reaching a hand to help her up and out.

"I remember." As she stepped out of the cabinet, Creath's legs were trembling and her breathing looked labored. She let Joseph support her over to sit on the bed.

Despite the grave circumstances, Chrystabel couldn't help disliking the sight of his hands on another woman. It reminded her of how it had felt to have his hands on *her* a little while ago. She didn't want to share that feeling with anyone else.

Creath drew deep, calming breaths. "I'd forgotten quite how dark it is down there."

"We never closed the entrance before," Joseph said, sounding concerned.

"I cannot believe we used to play in there for *fun*." Creath held a hand to her chest, as if to slow her heartbeat. "Has he left?"

"For now." Joseph's fists clenched. "He said he'd bring men to search the castle if he hasn't found you by Saturday."

All the color drained from her face. "Oh, God."

Lady Trentingham moved closer. "We'll make sure you're gone by Saturday, dear." She reached to pat Creath's shoulder. "That's four days from now. Surely the weather will improve by then."

Creath just nodded, as if she hadn't really heard.

Chrystabel had to sympathize with the girl, even if Joseph *had* just been touching her. "Are you really betrothed to that awful man?" she blurted out.

"Yes." The girl choked back a sob. "I hadn't any choice in the matter. Believe me, if I did…"

Chrystabel's heart squeezed. How devastated would she feel at being forced to marry a man she didn't love—let alone one as odious as Sir Leonard?

Lady Trentingham sat and wrapped an arm around the anguished young woman. "Our dear Creath grew up on the neighboring estate," she told Chrystabel and her siblings. "Her parents and only brother died of smallpox last year, and her father's brother was killed in the war, so a distant cousin of her father's inherited the baronetcy. And Sir Leonard Moore assumed Creath's guardianship, as well."

"*And* he was made a Justice of the Peace," Joseph put in with a look of disgust. "A post awarded to him by his Parliamentarian cronies. He boasts that he has the ear of Cromwell himself."

"The man enjoys power," Matthew said softly.

Lord Trentingham grunted. "And he wields a fair bit of it in these parts."

"So do you," his wife reminded him. "You're the most prominent lord in the county."

He snorted. "Once swords and pistols are drawn, I think you'll find my prominence offers little in the way of physical protection."

"Pray pardon," Chrystabel said, "but won't the castle provide physical protection? Are not castles built for the purpose of defense?"

Matthew rolled his eyes. "We live in modern times, Chrys, not the Middle Ages. Lord Trentingham cannot simply sound the trumpets and summon his knight-vassals to the battlements."

Chrystabel's face heated. "I didn't mean—"

"Besides which," Arabel chimed in, "given its large windows and lack of proper fortification, Tremayne is plainly not a true castle. Isn't that so?" She glanced up at Joseph expectantly.

"Quite so," he replied, looking impressed.

"Tremayne was intended to be a palace within a defensive castle," Lord Trentingham added. "But the outermost walls were never finished, the bastions and turrets never furnished with cannon armament."

"Very interesting," Chrystabel told him distractedly. She was still focused on her own blunder, followed by Joseph's reaction to her sister's astute observations. Did Joseph admire Arabel's intelligence? Did he think she was smarter than Chrystabel?

Did he *like* her better than Chrystabel?

That couldn't be, she assured herself. All of Arabel's knowledge came from books. Chrystabel had knowledge of a different sort—she knew how to read people.

Kneeling beside Creath with an air of tender concern, Matthew offered her his handkerchief. "Fear not, Mistress Moore, we won't let that old blackguard anywhere near you."

She accepted the square of linen, gazing up at him with leaking green eyes. "Thank you, my lord," she whispered reverentially—then looked away. "But please don't put yourself at risk. I've brought enough trouble upon this household already. I couldn't bear it if you—that is, if *any* of you came to harm."

"It's not your fault the bastard is determined to have you," Joseph said, beginning to pace. His short patience suggested they'd had this argument before.

Sighing, Matthew straightened. "Then I gather Sir Leonard knows his bride is unwilling?"

"Oh, I believe I've made my feelings more than clear," Creath said with a grim edge. "But he doesn't care. It isn't me he's after, anyway, it's the rest of my family's holdings. The baronetcy's entail carried a little land, but the bulk of the estate came through my mother to me."

Matthew's brow furrowed. "Whatever his motivation, he cannot lawfully force your consent."

"Actually, he can." Joseph's agitated pacing continued unabated. "As her guardian, he has the right to decide whom she marries—at least until she reaches eighteen next month."

"Then we must hide her until next month," Matthew persisted.

Joseph stopped and looked at him. "That's exactly what *we*"—he gestured to indicate his family—"are doing, in case you haven't noticed."

"But Saturday—"

"By Saturday, she'll be far from here and safe. We have the situation under control, Lord Grosmont." Joseph's words were polite, but firm.

Matthew's lips thinned. After a moment, he nodded. "Very well."

When nobody said anything else for a while, Chrystabel took a deep breath. "Since Mistress Moore is safe for now, shall we resume dancing?"

"I think not," Lord Trentingham said. "I believe we've had enough excitement for one night. I suggest we seek our beds."

This time his wife didn't disagree, so everyone said their goodnights and went off.

The Ashcrofts went one direction, while the Trevors went another. Chrystabel wondered where Joseph slept. All but floating up the grand staircase, she remembered the feel of him pulling her close during the volta. His warm hands holding her securely. The effortless way he'd lifted her.

She released a blissful sigh.

"Is something amiss?" Arabel asked as they walked down the well appointed corridor.

"Nothing's amiss," Chrystabel assured her. "Absolutely nothing." Glancing at their brother over her shoulder, she pulled her sister into her chamber. "Goodnight, Matthew," she called merrily before shutting the door.

Arabel stared at her. "What has got into you?"

"I'm happy." Humming to herself, Chrystabel drifted over to the oriel windows. It was too dark to see out, but she knew the lovely Tudor gardens were just below. "I know poor Creath is distressed, but am I not allowed to be happy? I'm in love."

Arabel plopped onto one of the stuffed chairs. "You still believe that?"

"Of course. I'm even more in love than I was earlier." Feeling lighthearted like never before, Chrystabel twirled around the spacious room, her dull brown skirts billowing around her as she pretended she was still dancing with Joseph. "It's a pity Lord Trentingham is such a fust-cudgel. I wanted to dance some more."

The second time she twirled by, Arabel grabbed her arm. "Stop!" she said with a giggle. "You're making me dizzy."

Chrystabel was breathless. "I'm dizzy in love. I thought I was overtired when we arrived, but I think I could have danced all night. Touching Joseph felt like a dream. And he felt something when he touched me too, I'm sure of it. I'm going to wear a beautiful gown tomorrow, and he's going to fall in love with me."

Arabel looked skeptical. "But the two of you argued at supper. And he seemed awfully upset over Creath's trouble..."

"They're old friends, is all. He's worried about her, and now she has to go far away to escape that nasty old brute. Although..." At first, Chrystabel had been relieved by the news of Creath's impending departure, since the girl's troubles were distracting Joseph. But now she had a better idea. "Did you see the way Creath and Matthew danced together, gazing into each other's eyes?"

Her sister shrugged. "I didn't notice."

"Well, I did. There's something between them, I'm sure of it. I think they belong together."

Laughing, Arabel shook her head. "You're seeing love everywhere today. Did you drink too much wine?"

"I drank exactly the right amount of wine, and I'm telling you Matthew and Creath belong together. And don't you see?" Chrystabel plopped onto the chair opposite her sister's. "If Matthew marries her before Sir Leonard returns on Saturday, Creath will be safe."

Arabel's mouth fell open. "You're out of your mind."

"But it's the perfect solution!" Chrystabel couldn't believe she hadn't thought of it sooner. "Sir Leonard won't be able to force Creath to marry him if she's already wed to Matthew."

"But the two of them barely know each other. Besides, they can't be married by Saturday. They'd have to wait three weeks for the banns to be called—"

"No, they wouldn't. Cromwell made marriage a civil matter, remember? A Justice of the Peace could wed them tomorrow, if they wanted."

"That's absurd—they only met today! And Matthew's never talked of wanting to get married."

"But he will. I'll make sure of it."

"Ah, now you fancy yourself a matchmaker? Chrystabel, you've gone mad." Arabel leaned over the hexagonal table to place a palm on her sister's forehead. "I think you must be ill."

Chrystabel batted her hand away. "I'm far from ill. I've never felt better in my life. And yes, I think I must be a matchmaker, because I seem to know when people belong together. Matthew and Creath belong together, and I'm going to help them get together."

Arabel dropped back onto her chair with an exasperated groan. "You cannot make them fall in love."

"You think not?" Chrystabel smiled. She'd show her sister what she was capable of. "Watch me."

EIGHT

HEN **CHRYSTABEL** woke the next morning and realized it was Christmas Eve and she was staying with people who weren't celebrating Christmas, she wanted to burrow back under the covers and cry.

The stars seemed aligned against her. First, she'd lost her jewels and most of her other fine things, so Father could help finance the war. Then Father, too, had been taken from her. Next, Mother had left. After that, all of Chrystabel's favorite entertainments—plays, parties, music, and dancing—had been forbidden to her. Finally, her home had been stolen as well.

And now they were trying to take away Christmas.

It was too much. She'd given up so much already. She couldn't bear the thought of losing even one more thing.

Somehow, she'd have to change the Ashcrofts' minds.

Idly playing with the lion pendant she'd left sitting on her bedside table, she thought of her lovely garlands and wreaths, and all the hours she and Arabel had toiled making them. She thought about how she'd fretted over them all through their long journey. She thought about how they'd miraculously survived the harsh winds and rutted roads intact...

And how they would now be unceremoniously tossed out.

No!

Every year since she could remember, she'd made and hung Christmas decorations with her family. Now that Arabel and Matthew were the only family she had left, they had to keep the tradition alive together. Never again would she get to see Father burst into the great hall and light up at the sight of their handiwork, but she could think of him up in heaven, watching them and smiling.

And besides the wasted decorations, Yuletide simply shouldn't be ignored. No matter what the law said, that wasn't right. It was a tradition, and Chrystabel loved traditions—at least those that suited her—and Yuletide was her favorite tradition of all.

This was no time to stay abed and weep. Steeled by new resolve, she threw back the coverlet.

While she'd dined and danced last night, her maid, Mary, had unpacked enough of her things for a few days' stay. Opening the wardrobe cabinet, Chrystabel grinned to find the beautiful red brocade gown she'd been hoping to wear. Mary knew her well.

Though it wasn't a day dress, Chrystabel would wear it anyway. It put her in mind of Christmas—and if it had the same effect on others, perhaps it would help her case. Besides, she wanted the young viscount to see her in this gown, and the sooner the better; she couldn't bear to wait until tonight. It was trimmed with several deep rows of lace ruffles and displayed a lot more décolletage than Cromwell would approve of, which meant it was perfect. She was certain Joseph would find her irresistible.

Mary helped her dress, then arranged her hair—in luxuriant ringlets and silk ribbons, a vast improvement over yesterday's modest knot—while Chrystabel sat at the pretty dressing table with her precious store of cosmetics. Enjoying the cool sunshine filtering in through the amazing curved oriel windows, she reddened her cheeks and lips and darkened her lashes.

"The weather sure has improved," Mary said happily.

Sometime in the night, the savage storm had calmed. Beyond the windows, sunbeams sparkled on the snow beneath a cloudless blue sky. "It's a beautiful day for Christmas Eve," Chrystabel replied, glad she'd already settled the matter of their remaining at Tremayne through Christmas Day. Elsewise, her brother would want to take advantage of the favorable conditions to continue their journey—and ruin all of her hopeful plans.

Including her plans for Matthew himself. She had only a short time to figure out how to make him and Creath fall in love. Gazing out the windows, she decided a brisk winter stroll might just do the trick. On Christmas Eve day, what could be more romantic than a secluded woods blanketed in pristine, glittering white? She could see it now: Creath's cheeks would turn fetchingly pink from the chill, Matthew would move close to share his warmth, and then...

They would kiss! Chrystabel was sure of it.

She sighed with satisfaction, confident in her plan. They would kiss, and then they would fall in love. And Matthew would marry Creath, saving the girl from the odious Sir Leonard.

It could all be resolved before Christmas Eve supper.

When a knock sounded on the door, it was Arabel, looking lovely in a forest green gown with silver stars embroidered on its underskirt and silver tissue peeking through its wide, slit sleeves.

"I see you noticed how Lady Trentingham was dressed last night," Chrystabel said with an approving smile.

"Indeed. And I see you noticed as well." Arabel beamed back. "You look splendid, Chrys. We're in red and green. It's beginning to feel like Yuletide!"

"It certainly is. Mary?" Chrystabel looked to her maid. "Please inform Thomas Steward that I'd like to have all the Christmas greenery unpacked and brought here to my chamber."

"Of course, milady."

Taking one last look in the mirror, Chrystabel tweaked her bodice to make the wide neckline perfectly frame the swell of her décolletage. Then she turned and took her sister's arm. "Shall we breakfast?"

As they quit the room, Chrystabel realized she was humming

again, her morning bout of melancholy all but forgotten. It always helped to have plans in place.

But Arabel was frowning. "Why did you ask Mary to fetch the trimmings? You know we haven't been given leave to decorate." When they reached the grand staircase, she withdrew her arm to lift her skirts.

"Worry not, dear sister." Beginning her own descent, Chrystabel swayed her hips, in case Joseph was watching. "Before breakfast is ended, we shall have leave to decorate and more."

Arabel's head jerked around to stare at her. "How will you accomplish *that?*"

Since she hadn't quite figured it out yet, Chrystabel felt a prickle of irritation. "Persuasion," was her vague answer.

"What makes you think you can convince them to change their minds?" her sister asked with obvious disbelief.

"You think I cannot?" Chrystabel lifted her chin. "Watch me."

Arabel just rolled her eyes.

Alas, the entry hall was deserted; Joseph must have gone ahead without them. By the time they found their own way to the dining room, everyone else was already seated.

"Good morning," Chrystabel sang.

A chorus of *good mornings* followed.

Lady Trentingham's gaze took in their altered style of dress. "My, how festive you both look!" She was dressed rather festively herself, in gold sarcenet with lace trim that looked like perfect, delicate snowflakes clinging to her shoulders and neckline. "Add but a strand of pearls, and you two would be ready for your presentation at court —if there still *were* a court."

"Oh, I adore pearls," Arabel cried. "But we haven't any. Father sold all our family's best jewels to support King Charles."

Chrystabel's eyes involuntarily met Joseph's. When his darted away, she knew he, too, had been reminded of their rather heated discussion last night. He looked a bit sheepish. Well, good. He ought to feel bad that his family had gone on prospering while hers had sacrificed so much. Although...

Well, he *had* made some good points. Perhaps Father could have been a *bit* more mindful of his family's future alongside his king's. Even after the war had taken a turn for the worse, he'd never talked about what would happen should the Royalists lose. Chrystabel suspected he'd never considered the possibility, let alone made provisions for it.

Feeling confused and flustered as she sank onto a chair, she allowed herself one deep, calming breath. There was much to accomplish during this meal. She couldn't afford to lose focus.

Perhaps it would be best to start with the simplest item first.

Buttering a hunk of bread, she favored Creath with a friendly smile. "Isn't it a beautiful day?"

"Aye." Though still a bit pale, Creath seemed in tolerably good spirits. "It's a perfect day for walking. I'm used to spending a good deal of time outdoors, but I've been stuck in this castle since I got here."

Ha! This would be even easier than Chrystabel had realized. She'd invite Creath to walk with her after dinner. Then, later, she'd invite Matthew along as well—and ultimately find some reason to excuse herself and leave the two of them alone.

Perfect. She opened her mouth to issue the first invitation.

"Your frustration is understandable, Creath." Joseph regarded her over the tankard of weak ale he had halfway to his lips. "But you know you cannot go outside."

Oh, hang it. Perhaps not so easy, then.

Creath nodded, looking resigned. "I know. It's just that this is the first nice day we've had in ages—but I'll make do with looking out the window. It's too dangerous to leave the castle," she explained to Chrystabel with forced good cheer. "I might be seen and my whereabouts reported to Sir Leonard."

Her mouth full of bread, all Chrystabel could manage was a sympathetic noise. She swallowed hastily. "Oh, but that seems extremely unlikely, given the dense woods all around. Why, this great big castle is scarcely visible from the road, so surely a small person—"

"It's not just those passing on the road who are a threat," Joseph interrupted. "The woods may belong to Tremayne, but there's no wall to keep people out."

Chrystabel raised a brow. "Do you often meet outsiders wandering about in your woods?"

"Never," Lady Trentingham answered for him. She seemed to be concealing a smile.

Joseph set his jaw. "It's still not worth the risk. Father, don't you agree?"

"Quite so."

Joseph's look was triumphant, as if that settled the matter.

But Chrystabel could be stubborn, too. "What if Creath were disguised?" she pressed.

"Disguised?" Joseph's smile was more than a little sarcastic. "It would have to be a *very* good disguise—"

"Never mind." There. As far as Chrystabel was concerned, she'd got Joseph's permission to take Creath on a walk as long as the girl wore a disguise. Now it was time for a quick change of subject— preferably something distracting—lest he catch on. She blurted the first thing that came to mind. "What does your family like to eat for Christmas Eve supper?"

"Pray pardon?" Well, she'd certainly succeeded in distracting him. He looked as though his eyes might pop out of his head. "We're not celebrating Christmas, remember?"

"My dear boy, do calm yourself," his mother teased. "I'm sure Lady Chrystabel was only making conversation. Weren't you, my lady?"

Chrystabel gathered her nerve. Though she still didn't have an actual plan for changing the Ashcrofts' minds about celebrating Christmas, she knew she could talk them around. Ever since she was a child, she'd always had an instinct about people. A special awareness. A way of sensing what others were thinking and feeling, of predicting how they'd react in different situations. In truth, if she trusted her instincts and really put her mind to it, she could talk most people around to most things—at least, most things that weren't counter to the individual's nature.

And her instincts told her that taking this risk wasn't counter to the Ashcroft family's nature. They'd bent the Puritan laws before— with their attire, winemaking, dancing, and other small acts of rebellion. This was only one step further.

"Actually, Lady Trentingham, I wasn't just making conversation. I was hoping you might allow me to plan a Christmas Eve supper, as well as a Christmas Day breakfast and a few other Yuletide activities, and to use the trimmings we brought with us to decorate your lovely home for the occasion."

"*Chrystabel*," her siblings said simultaneously—Arabel in an embarrassed groan and Matthew in a tone of warning.

Chrystabel took no notice. Her gaze was fastened on the lady of the house. Though she'd thought the countess enjoyed her company and might even approve of her proposal, Lady Trentingham didn't smile. But she didn't frown, either.

The woman did, however, raise a hand to keep her husband and son from interrupting. "You made a similar offer last night, Lady Chrystabel, which my husband declined. What makes you think you'll get a different answer this morning?"

She sounded interested, not accusing, which Chrystabel took as a positive sign. That left conservative Lord Trentingham and the over-cautious viscount as her main obstacles. The earl's resistance seemed to come more from an unthinking instinct for prudence than from genuine opposition, so she decided to see to him first. He ought to be easier to convince, and once both parents were on her side, they could help sway Joseph.

"Two reasons," Chrystabel told the countess, then turned to address Lord Trentingham directly. "The first being that I expressed myself poorly the first time. Last night, my lord, I spoke like one who eschews convention, respectability, and good sense for the sake of trifling frivolities."

Though he was too polite to agree, the earl mumbled something that wasn't a denial.

"Well, that couldn't be farther from the truth. I take the law quite seriously, and my rejection of it is not senseless but deliberate. I disobey out of respect for tradition and principle, just as you do by continuing to operate the vineyard you inherited from your father and continuing to dress in a manner that reflects your lineage and beliefs. Celebrating Christmas might be fun, but more importantly, in my opinion, it's our duty as Christians and an important way we honor and celebrate our faith and our families."

Everyone including Lord Trentingham looked a little stunned. After a protracted moment of silence, Joseph was first to find his voice. "I care about duty and tradition, too, but it's foolish to ignore the risks. One must strike a balance. The way you flaunt the law—"

"Who's flaunting?" Arabel wanted to know. "In public, Chrystabel dresses modestly and follows all the other restrictions. Even in private, she never drinks to excess and she hardly swears. And the small rebellions she does allow herself are always conducted discreetly in her own home—or the home of one she trusts. What's foolish about that?"

Pleased and touched, Chrystabel shared a smile with her sister. It felt good to have Arabel come to her defense. For once, her scholarly little sister had chosen to praise her judgment rather than challenge it.

But Joseph wasn't convinced. "What's foolish is taking unnecessary risks when we're already under scrutiny. Having Sir Leonard breathing down our necks increases both the odds of getting caught and the likely severity of retaliation. It's not a good time to push our luck."

"I agree," Chrystabel announced, and for a second time, everyone looked stunned. "That is, I agree lawbreaking should be avoided any time Sir Leonard is apt to show up unannounced—which is why I propose strictly limiting our observance to Christmas Eve and Christmas Day. I would make all of the arrangements myself and personally ensure the evidence is disposed of by midnight tomorrow, more than twenty-four hours ahead of Sir Leonard's return." When she locked eyes with the viscount, her heart gave its usual stutter despite their rivalry. "A brief, modest celebration would mark the holiday while incurring very little risk. Does that sound like a fair balance, Joseph?"

It was the first time she'd availed herself of his invitation to use his given name. Though she'd been calling him Joseph in her head since last night, hearing herself speak it aloud felt different and odd. But in a good way.

She wondered if he'd enjoyed hearing it. He certainly looked less belligerent than a few moments ago. Now he appeared surprised and intrigued, among other emotions she couldn't distinguish.

She liked the notion that he found her surprising. And he certainly seemed more interested in her now, though she wondered if that was partially thanks to the red gown. More than once, she'd seen his gaze lingering, well, not exactly on her face.

Could those other, indistinguishable emotions indicate burgeoning love?

Her heart gave a longer, harder stutter at the thought.

And when it became obvious he wasn't going to answer her question, she forgave him immediately. A man falling in love was bound to get a bit tongue-tied, after all.

Turning back to the others, she saw victory in her grasp. Creath and Arabel beamed, Lady Trentingham nodded eagerly, and Matthew shrugged his approval. Even Lord Trentingham looked a little excited. "All in favor?" Chrystabel asked.

When five voices said, "Aye!" Joseph seemed to come awake.

A rueful smile tugged at his lips. "Aye."

"Excellent!" Lady Trentingham dabbed at her mouth with her napkin and rose. "Lady Chrystabel, I'll leave you to planning our secret Christmas while my family discusses some issues of significance. Henry, shall we meet in your study in an hour?"

NINE

$\mathcal{T}$HERE WAS NO time to waste.

Chrystabel's schedule for the day quite suddenly seemed at least a mile long. Somewhere between her first bite of bread and her last sip of ale, she'd gone from having nothing to do to wondering how she could possibly get everything done.

After the meal, her first stop was the kitchen, where she surveyed what was available to plan her menus for Christmas Eve supper and Christmas breakfast. She squealed with delight when she found a basket of red fruit in the pantry.

"Strawberries?" she asked Mrs. Potter, the Ashcrofts' rosy-cheeked cook. "In the winter?"

"Oh, yes," Mrs. Potter said with a smile. "Lord Tremayne grows them in his conservatory."

"Does he?" Thinking she needed to see strawberries growing in winter, Chrystabel mentally added a visit to Joseph's conservatory to her long list of things to do today. "I think we should have a big strawberry tart. What else in your pantry can we use?"

Finding that the Ashcrofts had turkey, chicken, and bacon, she decided to have them baked into a large Christmas pie. Usually

Christmas pie also included goose and pigeon at a minimum, but she was certain the one she planned would be just as delicious.

She also found fish, cauliflower, and a basket full of small artichokes. Mrs. Potter had a number of fine ideas for employing those items, so Chrystabel left them to the cook's creativity. Fresh white manchet bread and a large sallet would complete the meal.

For Christmas breakfast, she examined the larder again and planned panperdy, buttered eggs with bacon, and hot pan cakes with butter and sugar.

"Do you have any red wine?" she asked Mrs. Potter. "Or do the Ashcrofts drink only the Tremayne wine here?"

"Oh, we have plenty of red wine in our cellar."

"Excellent. I hope you won't mind me invading your kitchen later this afternoon, because I'd like to make the mulled wine myself."

"You're quite welcome here, my lady," Mrs. Potter assured her. "We all have to look at each other most every day of the year, so we're always glad of a new face."

Chrystabel chuckled. "My heartfelt thanks." It took some tinkering and lots of tasting to make a perfect batch of mulled wine. She preferred not to risk leaving that task to a kitchen servant.

The mulled wine would be for tonight. What to prepare for a morning drink? Something sweet and delicious, as it was the most special of holidays.

"I don't suppose you have cocoa beans?" she ventured, her fingers worrying her lion pendant. Parliament had banned chocolate as a sinful pleasure, but...

"I certainly do," Mrs. Potter admitted, proving Christmas was the season for miracles. "It's a modest little hoard, but I'm not saving it for anything in particular. Shall I have the beans ground for you?"

"Oh, that would be marvelous!" Chrystabel loved chocolate nearly as much as she loved secretly ignoring ridiculous Puritanical laws. "I'll have all our kitchen staff fetched here to help you. Thank you once again, Mrs. Potter. Until this afternoon," she said as a way to excuse herself.

Now it was time to start decorating. Although first, she needed to stop by her brother's chamber.

On her way upstairs, she wondered if Lady Trentingham was holding her family meeting yet. She was insanely curious to know what the countess meant to discuss with her husband and son, because the lady's carefully offhand manner had made her suspect it was something quite serious. And she'd long ago learned to trust her instincts in matters such as this.

Could the Ashcrofts be meeting to talk about Chrystabel and her siblings? Were they unhappy to have the Trevors foisted upon them? Maybe...but last night Lady Trentingham's invitation to stay had seemed sincere, and today she'd agreed to let Chrystabel plan a secret Christmas in their home. It didn't make sense.

So she had to keep wondering.

When she knocked on the door of Matthew's chamber, he came to greet her with a quill in his hand. Glancing past him, she saw several open account books on a table. His hair was sticking up in places, as though he'd been running his fingers through it.

Was he anxious about their finances? She hoped everything was all right—but she had no time to worry about anything like that today.

"May I borrow a hat?" she asked, craning around him to try and spot one. "Or are they all still packed away in the wagon?"

"I think John brought up one or two." John was his valet. "But why do you need a hat?"

"For Creath. I mean to tuck her hair up under it."

He blinked. "Why on earth should you want to do that?"

"You and I must go out walking to find a yule log for our secret Christmas. Creath said she longs for the outdoors, and if we disguise her as a boy, she'll be able to come with us. You're too tall to loan her clothes, but I'll beg some off the younger Cartwright boy." The Cartwrights were the two musically talented brothers in their household.

She expected Matthew to call disguising Creath a harebrained scheme, since he often berated her ideas—but instead he just looked concerned. "I didn't hear any of the Ashcrofts agree that you might disguise her."

She shrugged that off. "They didn't disagree, either. The viscount said it would have to be a very good disguise, and I will make sure it is."

"Very well, then," Matthew relented with suspicious speed, walking right over to the wardrobe cabinet to pull out a hat. "Let me know when it's time to leave."

He wasn't arguing? He wasn't criticizing? He was just looking forward to their walk?

She took that as a very good sign, indeed.

Now it was time to get to decorating, just as soon as she got one of her staff to locate the Cartwright boy.

When her bedchamber yielded no trace of Mary, Chrystabel groaned. She didn't have time for this. With a sigh, she went back downstairs. Hat in hand, she began to wander in and out of rooms, in search of one of the Trevor servants. Any of the Trevor servants. Anyone who knew the Cartwrights, so she could task someone else with finding the younger brother.

In the fourth room she tried, she came across Creath, seated with a book. The chamber was lined floor to ceiling with dark-stained wood shelves. Tremayne's library.

Since she *did* need to speak with Creath, she approached the young woman, who didn't seem to notice anyone was there, so involved was she in her book. "What are you reading?" she asked, put in mind of Arabel.

"Oh!" Creath startled a little and looked up, then turned to the book's first page. "'*Artemenes, or the Grand Cyrus*,'" she read aloud.

Chrystabel saw that the book was written by someone named Madeleine de Scudery, and underneath the title it said, *That Excellent Romance*. "Goodness, that sounds interesting." She didn't often read books, but then again, the Grange's library included nothing that could be called romance. "What is the book about?"

The girl's eyes lit up. "So far Cyrus Artemenes is searching for his love, Mandana. She was abducted by the king of Assyria, and then again by a man named Mazare." Up until now, Chrystabel hadn't seen Creath so enthusiastic about anything. She was obviously enjoying this book. "Mazare was found dying on a shore after a shipwreck, and Mandana was believed dead, too. But she hadn't perished—she was actually taken by the king of Pontus, who is now holding her captive."

"How many times can one woman be kidnapped?" Chrystabel wondered.

"Apparently at least three," Creath replied with a little smile.

Chrystabel was glad to see the story was taking Creath's mind off her troubles. Having troubles of her own, she thought a distraction like this might do her good, too. "May I borrow that book when you're done with it?"

"You can read the first volume now. This is the second one. But I don't know if you'll have time to finish the whole story before you leave."

Creath didn't know that Chrystabel wasn't leaving, of course. Once Joseph fell in love with her, she'd have plenty of time to finish reading this book and many more. "How many volumes are there?"

"Ten. The whole book is over thirteen thousand pages."

"Thirteen *thousand* pages? Oh, my. I shall have to think about that." Actually, she would have to forget the whole idea. Chrystabel doubted she'd read thirteen thousand pages in her entire lifetime, let alone in just one book. And she certainly had more important things to do right now.

And so would Creath, soon enough.

"I've borrowed this to disguise you as a boy," Chrystabel said, holding up Matthew's wide-brimmed Cavalier hat. "So you can come out walking."

"Out of doors?" Creath bit her lip, looking torn between guilt and longing. "I don't think I'm allowed."

"You're allowed if you're disguised," Chrystabel said blithely. "I obtained permission from the viscount."

"He said that?"

"He did. And we would so enjoy having you along."

"We?"

"My brother and I." Chrystabel watched closely for a reaction.

She needn't have feared missing it.

"Oh!" Creath turned pale, then pink, then managed to drop her book and lose her place. "I, um, I'd be delighted to accompany you and your brother." Her words came out muffled as she was doubled over, feeling for the book.

"Wonderful." Chrystabel had to resist shoving her whole fist in her mouth to stifle a laugh. "I shall borrow a boy's breeches for you, too." She eyed the girl dubiously. "Have you a suitable cloak?" At breakfast she'd noticed Creath was wearing the same tawny dress she'd worn the day before. And she still had yet to change clothes.

Straightening, Creath shook her head. "I ran away from Sir Leonard with nothing but this gown I had on."

Chrystabel had guessed as much. "Oh, but Arabel and I have plenty of clothes! Some in our rooms and much more in our luggage." Luckily, Creath looked to be a similar size. "After our walk, we'll find you an elegant gown to wear for Christmas Eve."

"Would you? Lady Trentingham's gowns are too small and short for me. You're so very kind, Lady Chrystabel."

"Oh, pish, it's nothing." She waved the hat. "Breeches and a warm cloak, then. I'm off in search of that slippery Cartwright boy."

Surely she'd find him soon. Or find someone else who could find him. And *then* she'd start decorating.

TEN

"**W**HERE'S CREATH?**"** Joseph asked when he entered his father's linenfold-paneled study and closed the door behind him. Glancing about, he frowned. "And where's Father?"

"Your father will be along any moment, dear." His mother waved him into the overstuffed leather chair beside hers. "As usual, Creath is in the library. The poor thing still seems shaken up from her narrow escape. I thought it best not to disturb her without reason."

"Without reason?" Joseph's frown deepened as he lowered himself to sit. "Then are we not discussing—"

"We *are* discussing, you and I. Your father will join when he arrives, and Creath will surely go along with whatever decision we make. Such an obliging girl, that one," Mother added in a different tone.

A tone that made Joseph rather suspect she hadn't meant it as a compliment.

Which made no sense. Creath's obliging nature was one of the things he liked best about her—she was so easy to get on with. He must have mistaken Mother's meaning. In any case, she was right about one thing: Creath *would* happily go along with whatever he and his parents decided.

Shrugging, he leaned back and relaxed into the comfortable chair. "I gather you wish to settle on my wedding date, now that the weather has broken. My preference is Friday, in order to see the deed done before Sir Leonard returns on Saturday. Better he finds us married rather than missing, don't you think? At that point he'll have no recourse."

"There's a third option," his mother said, tapping her chin.

"Oh?"

"Sir Leonard returns to find you neither missing nor married—and Creath, he never finds at all."

"I...pray pardon?" He lurched upright in his chair, thinking he couldn't have heard her right. "Are you suggesting we postpone the wedding, or—"

"I'm suggesting you forget it altogether." Mother released a heavy sigh. "The truth is I've had doubts about this scheme ever since you announced your betrothal. I know you wish to save Creath. We all want to help her. But this isn't the only way. Why sacrifice your own happiness when instead—"

"I won't be sacrificing my happiness," he said through gritted teeth. Why did both of the women in his life think he'd be sacrificing his happiness? "I've known Creath since I was ten years old. We're the best of friends."

"Precisely. You're friends. And as her friend, you ought to help rescue her, quite certainly. A friend would help facilitate her escape. A friend would help her find someplace to hide."

"Where?" Losing patience, Joseph took to his feet and began pacing. "You think Sir Leonard won't search our other properties? Or are you thinking to hide her with friends? Who do we know who would put a stranger's welfare above threats to their own family? Where do you imagine she'll be safe?"

"I don't know. Somewhere far away or unexpected or—Wales!" His mother's eyes suddenly brightened. "Send her to Wales with Lord Grosmont. The Trevors are good people, and Sir Leonard won't look for her there."

Joseph opened his mouth to argue...then closed it. His pacing stopped short as an incredible notion struck him.

Was it possible this wasn't such a bad idea?

Neither Creath nor the Ashcrofts had any ties to Wales, meaning Sir Leonard was unlikely to follow her there. And even if, somehow, he learned of Creath's whereabouts, the bastard would wield far less power in Wales than he did here. His authority was for the most part restricted to this corner of England. His ability to intimidate—and to corrupt—would be far more limited across the border.

And the Trevors *were* good people. Despite their short acquaintance, Joseph felt confident in trusting them. Lady Arabel was naught but clever and kind—she would make a good friend for Creath. Not as good a friend as *he* was, of course, but far from lacking. And Grosmont had proved himself a decent sort, especially with his efforts to comfort and protect Creath. No matter that the fellow's misguided persistence was irritating, the compassion beneath it was obvious and admirable.

Even Chrystabel, interfering and insufferable though she was, seemed to be worming her way into Joseph's good graces. Her impassioned entreaty this morning had revealed a new side to her. If she hadn't quite convinced him of the wisdom of celebrating Christmas, at least she'd proven her heart was in the right place...

...that place being her bosom, which his male brain was now visualizing in its enticingly low-cut, figure-hugging red brocade bodice.

And now he felt hot again. Holy Hades, what was happening to him? He was either running a fever or losing his damned mind.

Wrenching his thoughts from that bizarre and unsuitable topic, he realized Mother had taken advantage of his silence to continue arguing her point. "...you see it's perfect? Sir Leonard has no idea who they are. He never asked their names. If Creath remained in Wales but a month, well past her eighteenth birthday, you'd both be free of him."

"You know it's not that simple, Mother." With a fresh surge of annoyance, Joseph resumed his pacing. He'd explained all of this before, and he had always hated repeating himself. "She'd be free of his guardianship, but he might still force her submission. Only a legal marriage can fully free her from his grasp."

"Then let her marry someone else," his mother snapped. "She's pretty and has money and land, which means she'll have her pick of men."

"Then why on earth shouldn't *I* pick her?" Joseph stopped pacing again, his fists clenched at his sides. "I promised to marry her, and I'm a man of my word. And given that there aren't any other suitable young women in this godforsaken wilderness—"

"Really, Joseph?" Mother looked heavenward. "You're twenty years old. Far too old for this silly pretending."

Joseph's mouth went dry. "What do you mean?"

"There certainly *is* another suitable young woman." Mother's brows arched, daring him to name her. "The one who thinks we live in the wilderness."

"The one who thinks...you mean Lady Chrystabel?" he asked incredulously, licking parched lips. "Are you mad? You think she's suitable?"

His mother cocked her head. "I think she interests you in a way Creath never will."

"She doesn't interest me." Joseph's cheeks flamed, along with other parts of him he refused to acknowledge. "She irritates me."

Mother grinned. "Because she's impulsive, irrational, and irresistible?"

"Yes. I mean, no! She's not irresistible!"

His mother's eyes shone even brighter, as though she'd somehow taken encouragement from his flat refusal. "She's refreshing and delightful and will keep you on your toes, my dear boy. You need a woman like her. I adore Creath, but she won't challenge you. She's so terribly good-natured that she'll go along with whatever you want." When she pulled a handkerchief from her sleeve to dab at her eyes, he realized their brightness was the result of happy tears. "And while I love your father, I don't want to see you follow in his footsteps and become an old fust-cudgel." After blowing her nose, she managed a watery smile. "I want to see you with someone who questions convention."

Before Joseph could formulate so much as a thought, his father banged into the study. "What's going on?" he called out, thumping the door closed behind him. "Did you start the discussion without me?"

"Of course not." Mother wiped the last traces of damp from her eyes before favoring him with a pleasant smile. "Do sit down, dear, and let us begin. When do you think our son ought to take his lovely bride to Bristol?"

ELEVEN

HILE HANGING a wreath above the great room's enormous fireplace, Chrystabel watched her sister artfully drape garlands along the mantelpiece. "What shall we give everyone for Christmas?" she asked the top of Arabel's head.

"Everyone?" With quick, practiced movements, Arabel tied off a neat red bow. "I've only got gifts for you and Matthew."

Careful not to trip on her skirts, Chrystabel made her way down the ladder. "Well, I haven't even got that much," she grumbled.

Her order for two pairs of handsomely embroidered gloves should have been delivered yesterday—to Grosmont Grange. She'd been planning to scent Matthew's with musk and Arabel's with rose oil. But now her lovely gifts were probably warming the hands of some blasted Roundhead and his dreary wife, while Chrystabel was forced to ransack her own trunks in search of last-minute substitutes.

And now she was adding gifts for the Ashcrofts to her lengthy list of tasks.

She must be mad. After wandering about the house for ages, she'd finally come across a harried-looking Thomas Steward to send on her errand for boy's clothes. As a consequence, she and Arabel had begun the decorating far later than she'd intended.

"Do you think our hosts expect gifts?" Arabel asked dubiously. "They know we didn't intend to spend the holiday with strangers."

"I'm certain they have no expectations." Backing up to admire her handiwork, Chrystabel smiled. Perfectly centered. Though something was missing... "But it's Christmas! And the Ashcrofts are no longer strangers. They've been awfully kind to us."

"They won't have anything to give us in return."

Chrystabel shrugged. "They've already given us their hospitality, which is more than enough."

"Holly."

"Pray pardon?"

Arabel held out a handful of loose sprigs. "The wreath needs more holly."

Chrystabel grinned. "My thoughts exactly."

Her sister helpfully gathered Chrystabel's skirts to one side so her stockinged feet could find the ladder's rungs. It was their usual arrangement, since Arabel disliked heights.

"I'm at the top."

Arabel let go and stepped back. "It's very thoughtful of you, Chrys."

"What?" She leaned forward to tuck more holly in amongst the pine, making sure the red berries showed.

"I said," Arabel called up to her loudly, "it's very thoughtful of you!"

Chrystabel giggled. "I'm about three feet off the ground. I can hear you just fine. *What* is thoughtful?"

"Oh." Her sister giggled, too. "Your thinking of gifts for the Ashcrofts. I do believe you're right that we ought to show our appreciation—"

"Stop."

Arabel immediately jumped away. "Is it the ladder? Is it breaking?"

Chrystabel rolled her eyes. "No, but I'm glad to know that if it were, you'd run instead of catching me. Can you repeat what you were saying before?"

"That we ought to show our—"

"No, before that."

"That it's thoughtful of you to—"

"No, after that."

Finally getting it, Arabel groaned.

"Please? I may never get to hear you say it again."

"Oh, very well." Planting her hands on her hips, Arabel heaved a great, overburdened sigh. "I do believe you're right."

"How I love the sound of that." Chrystabel closed her eyes in feigned bliss. "And I do believe I may be the older sister, after all." Her eyes snapped open when something brushed her ear. "Well, that settles the question," she added with a laugh. "Only children pelt their siblings with holly berries."

As she backed down the ladder, another berry bounced off her arm.

"If you want to be the responsible sister," Arabel said, "perhaps I shall leave it to you to sort out all the gifts."

"Ha!" Safely on the ground, Chrystabel smiled up at her wreath. *Now* it looked perfect. "I was thinking of making perfume for Lady Trentingham and Creath." Yet another thing to find time for today: creating two new scents. "Any ideas for Lord Trentingham?"

"I've been told he enjoys studying foreign languages." Arabel seemed to be getting into the Christmas spirit. "If I can find where our library is packed away, I believe there is a set of histories written in Italian."

"Perfect! Especially since we cannot read those books anyway."

"Speak for yourself," Arabel said archly. "I do read a bit of Italian."

"Just don't read it aloud," Chrystabel advised. "Your accent is atrocious."

That earned her a whole cluster of flying berries, which landed plumb in her décolletage, startling a laugh from her. It was a silly thing, but soon Arabel joined in, and then neither of them could seem to stop laughing. Chrystabel realized it had been a long time since she'd laughed this much with her sister. It felt almost like a real Christmas, like she wasn't all that far from home.

Arabel hiccuped, then giggled some more. "I think you should wear those berries to supper. Right there where they are now."

"With a garland in my hair." Chrystabel wiggled her shoulders. "How could Joseph resist me then?"

"He wouldn't stand a chance. You'd be just like a Christmas present for him to unwrap. In fact, if you haven't found one for him yet—"

"Arabel!" Chrystabel clutched at her stomach. "I'm begging you, please don't make me laugh any more."

But then she thought about Joseph 'unwrapping' her, and the idea didn't seem so humorous. As she fished the berries out of her bodice, a vision of *his* fingers plucking the little cluster from between her breasts threatened to turn her legs to jelly.

Suddenly feeling flushed, she cleared her throat. "No need to concern yourself with Joseph. I will find a gift for him."

Her hand went into her pocket to play with her lion pendant while she thought. What should she give her future husband? It would need to be something truly special for their first Christmas together.

"Very well, I'll leave Joseph to you. Is that everyone, then?" Arabel ticked off the names on her fingers. "Lord and Lady Trentingham, the viscount, Creath, and then you, me, and Matthew."

Arabel was easy, since Chrystabel knew exactly which of her gowns—the marigold silk satin embroidered with golden swirls—her younger sister most coveted. She had only to wrap it up for her. "I still need something for Matthew."

"What can you possibly give Matthew that you didn't bring along? He owns everything we have with us."

"I'll think of something." Sighing, Chrystabel stepped back into her red-rosetted shoes and pulled another wreath off the stack. "I always do."

TWELVE

"*W*AIT." **STANDING IN** Tremayne's entry hall, Chrystabel tucked a strand of Creath's bright reddish-blond hair back under her dull brown cavalier hat. Or rather, under Matthew's dull brown cavalier hat. "There. You're perfect."

Creath smoothed her palms on the brown breeches Chrystabel had borrowed for her. "Do you really think I look like a lad?"

"From afar, you certainly do. And if someone looks closer, they'll see the rest of us are strangers to the area, so they'll have no reason to suspect you're one of the party. Besides, we won't be straying from Tremayne property—Lady Trentingham has assured me we'll be able to find a perfect yule log in their woods. Let's go."

Watkins opened the door with a bow, and Chrystabel stepped into the chilly fresh air. It was beautiful outside. Sunshine sparkled off the light dusting of snow in the inner courtyard, and the sky was a pure blue.

She'd been so cold when they'd arrived that she hadn't paid any attention to the layout of the castle—she'd just wanted to get inside. Now she saw the courtyard was bordered by three long connected buildings that formed a U-shape. The gatehouse with its portcullis was in the middle of the center building, with the upper floors spanning the area above it. She could tell which wing her family's rooms were in and figured the Ashcrofts must sleep in the third wing. The obviously unfinished portion of the castle would be where Joseph's conservatory was located.

The far end of the courtyard was open to the fields and woods. She headed toward the trees, her siblings following.

"Hold on," Creath called from where she still stood in the entry. "Since Arabel is coming along, shouldn't we invite Joseph, too?"

"No." Chrystabel turned back. "If he's with us and anyone sees us, they might connect you with him."

"But you said we're staying on Tremayne property. And that I look like a boy from afar."

Chrystabel sighed. "Very well, I'll ask him." Before the girl could say she'd ask him herself, she hurried back inside.

Not really knowing where she was going but wanting to look like she did, she headed into the third wing, following the path she'd seen Joseph and his parents take last night when they went off to bed. Once she was hidden around a corner, she waited a minute, then another minute, and a third minute to be safe. Then she turned and retraced her steps.

"Joseph is busy," she told Creath. "Working with his father. Let's go."

"All right," Creath said, apparently happy enough to go without him as long as he'd been invited.

Chrystabel celebrated silently, glad her ploy had worked. She had a sneaking suspicion that Creath and Matthew wouldn't fall in love with Joseph watching over their shoulders. Well, more than a sneaking suspicion, really. She was sure of it.

Joseph was far too protective of Creath.

Lifting her pretty red skirts to keep them from dragging in the snow, Chrystabel kept up a stream of happy chatter as they all tramped through the courtyard, across a field, and into the woods.

"Which is the widest tree trunk?" she asked. "Which will make the best yule log? We want it to burn through tomorrow at least."

"We didn't bring a saw," Matthew pointed out. "How on earth do you expect to cut a yule log?"

"Ladies don't saw down trees," she shot back. "And I don't suppose you'd like to manage it alone? We'll choose a tree and then go fetch a few brawny servants to cut it and haul the log back." She shivered theatrically. "My, it's cold, isn't it? Much colder than I expected."

Her eye catching Matthew's, Creath flushed and huddled into her borrowed brown cloak. "I'm warm enough."

"Well, I'm not." Chrystabel faked another shiver, hoping she was giving a more convincing performance than Arabel had yesterday. "Why didn't I choose my heavier cloak? I believe I shall return to the castle for it." She looked to her sister. "Arabel, would you be so good to as to accompany me?"

"I'd rather not—"

"Thank you, sister," she said, seizing her by the arm. "I'll feel much safer with a companion."

"My pleasure," Arabel said without grumbling, because she truly was quite a kind sister. And she never grumbled.

"You two go on searching without us," Chrystabel called to Matthew and Creath as she dragged Arabel off. "We won't be gone long!"

"You're not shivering anymore," Arabel pointed out when they were well on their way. "And it's not especially cold, not like it's been these past few days. Are you sure you want to walk all the way back and then all the way out here again?"

"Yes, I'm sure I want to walk all the way back. After that, I think I will decide I'm exceedingly busy." Which was true; they were still behind schedule.

Arabel stopped in her tracks. "What do you mean?"

"I mean I'm not going back out there." Chrystabel tugged on her sister's arm again to get her moving. There was no time to waste. "I mean I intend to leave Matthew and Creath alone in the woods so they will fall in love."

"You're out of your mind, Chrys. I swear, you'd feel right at home in

Bedlam!" When Chrystabel walked faster, Arabel struggled to keep up with her. "Sir Leonard will be back for Creath three days from now—do you really think you can get these two to fall in love and wed before then?"

"I really think so, yes. I think they'll take their time choosing a tree for the yule log, and then take even more time getting to know each other before they realize we aren't returning. And then I think they will kiss, and I hope they will fall in love. Or maybe they'll fall in love and *then* kiss," she added, unsure of the order in which these things happened.

Chrystabel had yet to be kissed. To her great distress, in all of her nineteen years the opportunity had never arisen. Most of the suitable young men back in Wiltshire had left years ago to fight for King Charles. And many of the *un*suitable ones had gone to fight against the king, while the remainder seemed too gutless to even talk to an earl's daughter, let alone kiss one. Which was a shame, because Chrystabel liked talking to all sorts of people, and might have liked kissing them, too, if given a chance.

From her older sisters' accounts and her own daydreams, she just knew that kissing would feel glorious. And kissing Joseph would be the best Christmas present imaginable. She could already feel his long arms enfolding her, smell his mouthwatering fresh scent, taste his... well, as it happened, taste was one area where her imagination failed her. She wondered how Joseph would taste—besides delicious, of course. Lips as full and soft-looking as his couldn't be anything less than delicious. She couldn't wait to taste them.

Just like when she was small, she wanted to open her Christmas present *now*.

Where would it happen? Since she did feel a little cold, she decided to imagine him kissing her for the first time before a roaring fire, perhaps in the great room. Heat from the flames warmed her skin, while heat from the kiss warmed—

"You're awfully confident for your first day as a matchmaker," Arabel grumbled even though she never grumbled.

Indignant at being yanked from her lovely Christmas daydream, Chrystabel raised her chin. "I ought to be confident. I'm good at this,

Arabel. You'll see." She glanced back as they crossed the field, pleased to note that the young couple appeared to have vanished into the woods. Her plan of dressing the fugitive all in brown had worked. Creath wouldn't be at risk.

Everything was going perfectly.

"I don't like it." Apparently Arabel didn't think everything was going perfectly. "It feels wrong to desert them when we said we would return."

"But *you* said nothing of the sort." The snow crunched beneath their shoes. "I will take the blame. You've no reason to fret, Arabel."

Arabel continued to fret anyway. "Matthew will be furious. They might be out there for hours, waiting for us, worrying that something might have happened to us. We have to go back!"

Instead of turning around, Chrystabel walked even faster. "I'm not going back, and I'm not letting you go back, either. There's far too much to do. We need to finish decorating before we can make perfume for the ladies. I need you to add garlands to the grand staircase while I hang wreaths in the dining room and library."

And she'd also take a wreath to Joseph's conservatory, she added silently. Not that his indoor garden needed decorating, but now that she knew where it was, she was eager to pay a visit. And who could fault her for mistakenly wandering into the wrong part of the castle in the midst of her wreath-hanging fervor?

Nobody. It would look like a perfectly innocent blunder.

Would he kiss her in his conservatory?

"Chrystabel, are you even listening?" When they reached the inner courtyard, once more Arabel rudely interrupted her thoughts. "You cannot leave Matthew and Creath out there alone!"

"You think not?"

"Let me guess," Arabel groaned. "You want me to watch you."

THIRTEEN

*J*OSEPH WAS PLANTING flowers when Chrystabel walked into his conservatory.

In the diffused light from his parchment-covered windows, wearing her government *un*approved red gown, her cheeks flushed with holiday excitement, she suddenly looked different.

She suddenly stole his breath away.

Holy Hades, had his mother been right?

No. She'd put ideas into his head, that was all. Ideas he needed to reject.

Chrystabel was carrying a Christmas wreath. Determined not to betray his thoughts, Joseph restricted his reaction to a single raised brow. "Surely you don't need to decorate in here."

"No, no." Her smile was entirely too charming. "I arrived in here mistakenly."

And he was the Royal Gardener. "You wandered into this half-built wing thinking it was part of our living quarters?"

"Yes," she said, a brazen lie that he found inexplicably charming as well.

He needed air, and he needed to come to his senses. Even though he'd gathered enough pots for his seeds already, he crossed to the wall where he kept stacks of them and fetched an empty one back to his bench, using the time to draw several deep, steadying breaths.

His head felt clearer when he returned. She was still standing there smiling. She'd set her wreath on the floor. "You have an enormous space here."

"Indeed." Entire wings tended to be enormous. "Shall I show you back to the main house?"

She glanced about, her wide-set chocolate-brown eyes bright with curiosity. "Would you mind if I have a look around first?"

He wanted to say, *Hell yes, I'd mind*, but that would be impolite. So instead he said, "By all means."

Through gritted teeth.

In an effort to take his mind off her, he went to one of the fireplaces and chucked another log inside. She'd said she wanted to look around, but she wasn't looking around. She was looking at him. He wasn't looking at her, but he could feel her gaze on his back.

"What are you doing?" she asked.

"Building up the fire to keep my plants warm."

"I meant, what were you doing before that? When I came in."

"Oh." With a sigh, he turned to face her. "I was planting chrysanthemums."

"Chrys—what?"

"Chrysanthemums. My favorite flower." She wasn't letting him take his mind off her, damn it. And he didn't have the fortitude to rebuff a girl who might be interested in his flowers. "Come, I have mature chrysanthemums over here."

She followed him to the other end of his conservatory, where dozens of them were growing in wooden boxes. "Oh, they're beautiful!"

"Thank you," he said, her obvious delight making him smile. He was very proud of his chrysanthemums. He had pinks and whites and greens and reds and purples and oranges. A few were two-toned; those were his favorites.

"I've never seen anything like them," she breathed, circling the boxes to examine each color.

"They're very uncommon here—in fact, I may be the only one growing them. They just recently arrived on the Continent from China."

"How did you get them?"

She looked truly interested, which made him eager to tell her. "My uncle left England years ago, when King Charles first went into exile. Even as a small child I loved growing things, and he never had a son of his own, so he indulges me, sending me plants I cannot find here. I'm very fortunate."

Finished with her circuit, she knelt beside him to inhale the flowers' fragrance, her elegant red gown pooling around her. "Oh, their scent is strong, quite earthy and herby. Perfect to temper the sweeter flowers."

He swallowed hard. His position above her treated him to a view down the front of her close-fitting bodice. The sight of two half-moon swells of smooth, ivory skin was almost more than he could bear. On her slender frame, those breasts looked soft and devastatingly feminine.

He wished he could see more of them. His heart was pounding, and he was beginning to feel hot. For a moment he felt nearly as out of breath as he had dancing the volta last night. Remembering the huge, dowdy Puritan collar he'd wanted to rip off her, he longed for its return.

Because now he found himself wanting to rip off her entire gown.

Bloody hell, what was happening to him?

When she sighed, her bosom rose and fell in the tight bodice. His whole body clenched. "I wish I were going to be here long enough to make some of these into essential oil," she said wistfully.

He backed away a step, struggling to refocus on the conversation. "Make chrysanthemums into oil? Why would you do that?"

"So I can use the oil to make perfume." She looked adorable looking up at him. "I'm a perfumer."

"That's right, you mentioned it at supper. I'd never thought about someone creating all those fragrances people wear."

He wasn't thinking about that now. In fact, he was having a hard time thinking about anything but her enticing décolletage, and how it would feel to—

No. He was *not* having these thoughts. He was marrying Creath in two days, for heaven's sake. He could not allow himself to be consumed by lust for another woman.

Unable to stand the tempting sight a moment longer, he found her hand and pulled her to her feet. A little frisson of excitement bolted through him at the contact, but he determinedly ignored it. "Did your mother teach you how to make perfume?"

"My mother taught me very little." She frowned momentarily but quickly brightened. "My father's sister lived with us when I was a girl. Aunt Idonea taught me how to distill oils from flowers and mix them to make perfumes."

The discussion involved flowers, so even though he desperately wanted her to leave, he couldn't help but continue it. "Which flowers do you use?"

"Every type I can find—all of those that are scented, I mean. Plus some plants that have scent but don't flower. My favorite scent is rose, though." She glanced around. "I don't see any roses. I guess you can only grow roses outdoors?"

"I think I could probably grow them indoors in winter, but we haven't any roses here at Tremayne." Happily, he felt more in control with her standing. She was tall enough that he couldn't see down her bodice. "We do have roses at Trentingham. Or at least we did—I have no idea what Trentingham's beautiful gardens look like now."

An adorable frown appeared on her brow. "Surely your caretakers are sustaining your roses for you."

"We have no caretakers at Trentingham anymore. Once we left, Cromwell commandeered it to use during the war."

"Blackguard," she muttered in a decidedly unladylike way.

She was refreshingly outspoken. And he was intrigued to find she not only loved flowers as much as he did, she actually *used* them for her pastime. Her enthusiasm for perfuming seemed to be as strong as his for growing things.

All at once, he wished he were growing flowers *for her*.

And even worse, he wished he weren't marrying Creath.

He wondered if he might be falling in love.

But that was absurd. He barely knew Chrystabel—a relevant fact in itself—but he knew enough to know they were wrong for each other. Here was yet another *i* word: incompatible. How could a fellow as cautious as he fall for a girl as reckless as Chrystabel?

And in any case, a man couldn't fall in love in one day. He wasn't falling; he was reacting to the sight of luscious breasts—and to the ideas Mother had put in his head. All her talk of delightful this and refreshing that had shaken him.

No matter what his mother said, Chrystabel *wasn't* irresistible.

He was just finding her hard to resist.

But resist he must, because an innocent young woman was counting on him. He couldn't think of anything that would be more dishonorable than abandoning his best friend.

While he'd mused about love and honor and cleavage, Chrystabel had been wandering his conservatory, examining the plants here and there. "Strawberries!" she exclaimed now. "I've been wanting to see where you grew them." She paused in the middle of reaching for one. "May I?"

"Of course."

She plucked it and popped it into her mouth. Strawberry red fruit between her strawberry red lips—the vision was shockingly sensual. "Mmm," she murmured appreciatively. "I cannot wait for strawberry tart tonight."

He couldn't wait to watch her eat more strawberries.

And now he wanted to kiss the strawberry juice off those tempting strawberry red lips.

He was pathetic.

She wandered over to his next planter box and bent to sniff the small flowers there, treating him to another view. He quickly averted his eyes.

"Oh! I've never smelled this scent before. It's lovely." With obvious delight, she ran her fingers over the delicate white petals. "What kind of flower is this?"

"Those are potato plants," he told her, still trying to get the image of kissing her out of his mind. "The fact that they're flowering means the potatoes are ready to be harvested."

"Harvested?" She straightened—to his great relief—and cocked her pretty head to one side. "You don't grow these for the flowers, then? What's a potato?"

"It's a tuber—a much-thickened underground part of the stem. It bears buds from which new plants grow, and it also serves as food for the plant. And it's a good food for us." He knelt down and dug around one, then pulled it out and rose with it. "You can eat it."

It was brown, lumpy, and covered in dirt. She grimaced.

He found that grimace charming.

Which was not the same as delightful.

"It's ugly," she said.

"It's delicious."

"I've never heard of a potato before."

"They aren't common in England. They're from the New World. My uncle sent me my first few plants, and they're easy to grow, so now I have many. A whole field of them in growing season—it's one of our crops. I planted these in here so we wouldn't run out over the winter."

"You really like to eat them, then." She licked her lips, sending a stab of hot lust through him. "Are they eaten raw or cooked?"

"Not raw!" He laughed, which made him feel a little less hot. Or maybe it made him feel a little less lust. Whichever, he felt better. "They taste awful raw," he added with more than a little relief. "Our cook prepares them many ways, but my favorite is a pudding with lots of butter and spices."

"Can we have some tonight? I love trying new things."

She suddenly struck him as the kind of girl who would try anything. The thought filled him with unwelcome excitement. The image of kissing her was gone—well, faded, anyway—but his heart was galloping regardless.

Bloody hell. What on earth was he going to do about this? It wasn't right. He'd never felt so disloyal and despicable in his life.

"Of course we can have some tonight," he forced out through gritted teeth. "Let me dig up more, and I'll take them to the kitchen."

FOURTEEN

*S*EATED THREE HOURS later at the pretty hexagonal table in her bedchamber, Chrystabel cocked her head. "If you're sure there's no lavender, rosemary should do."

A knock sounded only seconds before Matthew opened the door.

"Uh oh." Arabel's eyes widened as she handed over the vial of rosemary oil. "I warned you," she whispered, "he's going to be furious."

But Chrystabel hadn't been worried, and she wasn't worried now. When Matthew approached, one look at his face told her he was *not* furious, although she suspected he'd pretend he was for a while.

She knew her brother.

"You said you were coming back," he scolded, just as she'd expected. "Why didn't you come back?"

"I was awfully cold, and I realized I had too much to do." Wearing her best mask of blithe innocence, she unstoppered the vial and took a delicate sniff. "I had to finish decorating, and now I'm making perfume for gifts. And I still have to oversee Christmas Eve supper. Did you find a good tree to cut for the yule log?"

"Yes. That took us only a few minutes."

Purposely delaying her reply, she made a note on a little card before dipping her dropper into the rosemary oil. She'd run out of lavender oil, but the rosemary would add a lovely lavender-like top note to the scent she was creating for Lady Trentingham. "If finding the log took only a few minutes, then why did you and Creath take so long to return?"

"Maybe because we were waiting for you?"

She peeked up at him through her lashes. "Or maybe not?"

Shying away from her knowing gaze, he skirted the table and wandered over to the curved oriel windows. Then he just stood there, looking down on the snow-blanketed Tudor gardens in silence.

She added two drops of the rosemary oil to her bottle and swirled it gently. "Spill it, Matthew."

"I don't know what happened." He remained facing away, his warm breath fogging the glass as his words tumbled out in a rush. "We talked and talked. And walked and talked some more. It was cold, but I didn't care, and she didn't seem to, either. I think I could talk to Creath forever and never run out of things to say. I just met her yesterday, yet I feel I've known her for years."

Chrystabel's mouth hung open. Never in her life had she heard her brother speak this way about a woman—or speak about women at all. Not in front of his sisters, anyway. Though her heart soared, she made no response. Instead she sniffed her concoction, decided she was pleased, and corked it. One more gift crossed off her list.

Passing over another empty bottle, Arabel's big brown eyes flashed with disbelief and excitement.

Chrystabel couldn't suppress a grin. Thankfully, Matthew couldn't see it.

She forced herself to focus on the bottle. "Creath is sweet, don't you think?" she said conversationally, using a little silver funnel to add alcohol and water from two pewter flagons. "I think a floral scent will fit her. Orange blossoms, and maybe some vanilla. Lilac, I think… Arabel, do you see lilac oil?"

Arabel searched the rows of vials with their tiny, neatly lettered labels. After handing over the requested lilac, she looked to her brother's turned back. "Did you kiss Creath?" she asked bluntly.

Matthew's shoulders tensed, but he said nothing.

"Chrystabel said you would kiss her. She also said you two would fall in love. Are you two in love, Matthew?"

"Hell, no," he ground out, sounding miserable. "Maybe I did kiss her. But if I did, it was a mistake. It was—" With a strangled noise, he cut himself off. His head drooped, his forehead banging into the glass. "Anyway, she hated it. She ran away right after, even though things had been going so well."

Chrystabel's insides churned with shock over his candid admissions and sympathy for his hurt and confusion. She'd never seen him fall to pieces like this before. He'd scarcely ever appeared less than composed and in control.

But besides all that, she couldn't help feeling a stab of childish envy, too. Matthew had kissed seventeen-year-old Creath, and yet she, nineteen-year-old Chrystabel, still had yet to be kissed.

How unfair was that?

"I suspect she was just startled," she told her brother. "You took her by surprise. Her new feelings took her by surprise."

He finally turned from the windows, his dark eyes glazed. "She wasn't the only one taken by surprise."

"Of course you're both surprised. Your feelings grew very swiftly. But just think, Matthew—you can save her from that awful Sir Leonard! If you marry her before he returns, she'll be safe from his fiendish designs. You can be her knight in shining armor like in days past." She gave a romantic sigh. "You must marry her, and quickly."

Now it was his turn to look shocked. "Marry her? I just met her! And my whole life has just been turned upside down. I'm being forced to move to Wales and start over, and I…I cannot begin to contemplate marriage, not on top of everything else."

"I know the timing isn't ideal." Adding three drops of lilac to Creath's scent, Chrystabel set down the bottle to fix her brother with an earnest gaze. "It's true the two of you just met, but some things are meant to be. Not every man is lucky enough to meet his perfect match. Don't you see that you have to act now, or she'll be lost to you forever? She'll be married to Sir Leonard and having his babies instead of yours."

"Babies? One kiss and you're talking babies? I cannot listen to this." Matthew stomped to the door.

"Where are you going?" Arabel called after him.

"Away!" he growled. "To see that our servants cut and haul the yule log for your deranged sister's illegal secret Christmas."

The door slammed behind him.

"He wasn't furious," Chrystabel pointed out to her sister calmly.

"He is now."

"He'll get over it. Can you pass me the vanilla?"

Arabel didn't. "I think you were right about Matthew and Creath," she said slowly, tracing one of the stars embroidered on her gown. "He's in love, even I can see that. And your plan brought them together—at least for a little while." She met her sister's gaze with reluctant awe. "Perhaps you *are* a bit of a matchmaker."

"It would seem so," Chrystabel said modestly, not wanting to appear smug. Though she *had* known she was right all along. "Matthew will sort things out with Creath, I'm sure of it. All that's left now is to secure Joseph's heart for myself. I've decided what to give him for Christmas."

"A bottle of scent?"

Searching for the vanilla herself, Chrystabel shook her head. "Not a bottle of scent."

"Why not? Men wear perfume too, you know."

"Not Joseph. He likes growing flowers, not wearing them."

"How do you know?"

"You think I don't know the man I'm going to marry?"

Arabel laughed. "So what are you going to give him?"

"My roses." Just saying it aloud filled her with anticipation. She couldn't wait to see his reaction.

"What roses?" Arabel paused in thought. "You can't mean *your* roses—"

"*My* roses," Chrystabel confirmed. "He grows flowers, and he doesn't have any roses here at Tremayne. They're the perfect gift for him."

"But you love those roses—you fought tooth and nail to bring them along. Lord, I thought you would rather have left Matthew behind than those bushes! Why on earth would you give them away now?"

"You're not seeing the situation clearly," Chrystabel said, adding two drops of vanilla to the bottle. "Joseph will have my roses, but I will have Joseph. He'll care for them, I'll have my essential oils, and we'll live happily ever after."

"Oh, Chrys…" Concern in her eyes, Arabel cleared her throat. "You know happily ever afters only happen in fairy tales. Shouldn't you lower your expectations, at least a little? Elsewise you're bound to be disappointed."

"I disagree. I think I'm destined for a happily ever after, and so are you. After Joseph and I get married, I'm going to find your match."

"Not that I'm convinced you can, but please don't. I'm not ready to get married."

Chrystabel swirled the bottle. "Whyever not? Being in love feels wonderful."

"But *making* love doesn't." Her sister bit her lip. "Don't you remember what Martha and Cecily told us?"

"Oh, pish, they said it only hurts the first time. You cannot avoid marriage just because you're worried about *that*," Chrystabel told her, though she sometimes worried about *that* a bit herself.

"I have no intention of avoiding marriage. I'm just not in any hurry, either."

"You will be when I find your perfect match. And then, once again, you will have to admit I was right. Now, smell this."

Arabel rolled her eyes—good-naturedly, because she was Arabel—and raised the bottle of perfume to her nose. "It's lovely. Creath will adore it."

"Excellent."

Arabel corked the bottle. "Are we done, then?"

"With perfuming. But there's still so much to do." Rising, Chrystabel took out her penknife and went to the wardrobe cabinet. Opening it, she pulled a dress forward and cut off half of a hook-and-eye fastener.

Arabel gasped. "Why on earth did you do that?"

"I need something that looks like an anchor." Chrystabel handed her the little hook. "Don't you think this resembles an anchor?"

"A little, I suppose," Arabel said doubtfully. "What's it for?"

"For a pudding token."

"Oh!" Arabel's eyes lit up. "We're having Christmas pudding tonight?"

"Well, no. Tremayne's staff was told not to make any beforehand, and it's too late to begin now. We're having strawberry tart instead."

Arabel's pout looked out of place on her normally cheerful face. "Strawberry tart is a sad substitute for plum pudding."

"It's the best substitute we've got," Chrystabel retorted. "Plum pudding takes weeks to mature, and we have but a few hours. Anyhow, aren't you amazed that we're going to eat strawberries in wintertime?"

"That's certainly…exotic. And I'm sure the tart will be lovely. It just won't be Christmasy."

"But strawberries are red," Chrystabel persisted. "That's festive! And we'll still have the pudding tokens. It'll be plenty Christmasy, you'll see."

Her sister's shrug was noncommittal. "I wonder what happened to the plum pudding we made on Stir-Up Sunday."

"I tried to sneak it into the wagon, but Matthew caught me." As luggage space was limited, their brother had drawn the line at bringing sticky Christmas pudding with them to Wales.

Arabel sighed. "Such a waste."

"Not entirely. I left the pudding out on our kitchen worktable for whoever comes to claim Grosmont Grange. But first…" A tiny smile curving her lips, Chrystabel waited for her sister to look up. "First I doused the thing in vinegar and added enough pepper to choke an army."

While Arabel dried her tears of mirth, Chrystabel rummaged in her sparsely filled jewel box to find her daintiest ring. As she slipped one on and off her pinkie, her maid knocked and entered.

"Oh, there you are, Mary."

"Here's the thimble you asked for, milady."

"Just in time." Chrystabel tucked the ring and thimble into her pocket, together with the little hook. Her tasks here were finished. "Mary, do you think you could locate my store of fabric cuttings and bring it here? If you'll wait for her, Arabel, I'd like you to leave you in charge of the gift wrapping." On her way out, she paused before the fancy gilt mirror and tweaked her neckline back into place.

"Where are you off to?" Arabel asked.

"A meeting in the kitchen." Dipping her finger into a little pot, she smoothed berry-red pomade over her lips.

For this particular meeting, she wanted to look utterly kissable.

FIFTEEN

*H*AVING **NO IDEA** why he'd been summoned to the kitchen late that afternoon, Joseph was on his way when he passed the library and decided to take a detour.

As he'd expected, Creath was inside. But for once she wasn't reading. A book lay open and forgotten on her lap while she stared at the dancing flames in the fireplace.

"What's wrong?" he asked, startling her from her reverie. "What are you thinking about?"

A vague expression clouded her face. She still seemed preoccupied. "Well, you know I went for a walk, and—"

"You *what?*" All the air seemed to have left his lungs.

"I walked. You knew I was going to."

"I most certainly did not."

A little crease appeared between her brows. "Yes, you did. Chrystabel disguised me as a boy, which ended up not mattering because no one saw us."

He might've known Chrystabel was behind this. More proof of the recklessness that made her unsuitable. More reason to avoid her—and disturbing thoughts of her—at all costs.

He pulled a deep breath into his now-functioning lungs. "Thank God you weren't seen."

She managed to wave off his concern while still looking concerned herself. "That's not what I was thinking about. It's just...well...I guess things felt different out there." She looked away from him, back toward the fire. "And ever since, I've been thinking about how you shouldn't marry me. About how it really wouldn't be fair to you."

"Not that again." He was tired of having this argument with both her and his mother, but he wouldn't berate Creath when she was looking so anxious. Instead, he chucked her under the chin. "You can't change my mind, sweetheart. Not now that I've finally got used to the idea. I'm afraid you're stuck with me. Forever."

"Are you sure?" she asked wanly.

"I'm sure," he said, and if a vision of Chrystabel seemed to flash across his vision, he knew better than to pay it any mind. "Are you all right?"

"I suppose so. Yes, I'm fine." Mustering a small, brave smile, Creath picked up her book. "Do feel free to go about whatever it was you were doing."

"I've been summoned to the kitchen. I dug up twenty potatoes earlier, but I suspect they want more."

"I like potatoes."

"Me, too. See how compatible we are?" Glad to see her familiar smile widen, he considered giving her a kiss for reassurance. But he didn't feel like it just now. "Enjoy your book," he said instead on his way out.

Everything will be fine, he told himself as he continued on toward the kitchen. *It's going to be fine.* Creath was loyal and steady and a good friend, and theirs would be a pleasant, serene marriage. Young people of his class rarely had the luxury of wedding for love—or lust, for that matter—so marrying for other reasons was no great sacrifice. He could easily have faced a much worse choice.

Or had no choice at all.

Reaching the enormous kitchen, he found it crammed with Ashcroft and Trevor servants, all of them hard at work. Given the last-minute decision to celebrate Christmas, he wasn't surprised. But he *was* surprised to find Chrystabel there, too.

Surprised and none too pleased. Aside from wishing to avoid her in general, he was specifically vexed that she'd put Creath at risk by taking her out for a walk.

"What are *you* doing here?" he burst out peevishly.

"Tasting the potato pudding," she said, perfectly pleasant in the face of his rudeness. That was vexing, too. "Your potatoes are delicious, Joseph! You truly are a marvel."

He liked the way her lips formed his name, as though clinging to each syllable. Once again, he found himself wanting to kiss those lips. And he couldn't help liking how she always made him feel good about himself. He didn't know whether she was loyal and steady like Creath, because he didn't know her at all, really. But she was certainly enthusiastic and warmhearted.

And adorable, not to mention desirable, tied into a pretty cutwork apron that cinched her trim waist but stopped short of obscuring her enticing décolletage. Standing at the big wooden worktable over a bowl of potato pudding, she slowly licked the spoon clean.

Now he wanted to kiss potato pudding off her lips.

He found himself moving closer, unable to stop himself. She was a paradox. Though everything she did seemed calculated to arouse him, she had an air of innocence about her as well.

Another damned *i* word, he thought, cursing his mother silently.

"Mmm," Chrystabel hummed, her contented noises conjuring up the worst sort of disturbing thoughts. "Whoever would have thought those ugly brown things could make such a savory pudding? Come, you must try some. We used onions, cloves, and nutmeg—"

"Thank you," he snapped, "I'm not hungry." Then he felt instantly ashamed of his rudeness. He was lashing out at Chrystabel, when in truth he was just angry with himself for being a faithless, lascivious worm.

Well, he was a *little* angry with Chrystabel—for taking Creath on a walk and for wearing that damnable red gown with its low-cut, tight bodice—but that was no excuse to act ungentlemanly. It seemed he couldn't keep his head on straight whenever Chrystabel was near. He needed to finish his business here so he could leave the kitchen and go back to avoiding her.

"My valet told me I'd been summoned here," he told her, "but he didn't know why. Do you know if Mrs. Potter needs more potatoes?"

"Thank you, but we have plenty," Mrs. Potter said, bustling by.

"I agree." Chrystabel gestured toward the large bowl of potato pudding. "This dish seems to be quite enough for all of us, don't you think? I asked you here to—"

"*You* asked me here?"

"Yes, I was hoping you'd help me make some mulled wine. My family always drinks mulled wine while we sing carols on Christmas Eve."

"Then wouldn't you rather make it with your family? Why don't you ask your sister or brother to help?"

"I've set them to doing other tasks." Two kitchen servants deposited a massive strawberry tart on the worktable. "Matthew is seeing to the yule log, and Arabel—"

"How about Creath?" he interrupted. "You could ask Creath. She's just sitting in the library."

"I went to ask her, but she looked a little sad. She seems happier with a book."

Chrystabel was perceptive. Which should be a positive trait, but today it only annoyed him. He gritted his teeth—he found himself doing that a lot around her. "I've never made mulled wine. What makes you think I can help?"

"Anyone can help. It's easy."

Anyone could help, but she'd asked *him*. What had he done to deserve this temptation? It wasn't right to feel tempted by Chrystabel when he had to marry Creath.

He could only thank his lucky stars that at least she wasn't kneeling down or leaning over. Maybe they could get this done quickly, so he could leave here relatively unscathed.

"Let's get started, then," he said. "We'll need to get some wine from the cellar."

"So Mrs. Potter told me. But I was just about to hide some tokens in the strawberry tart, since we don't have plum pudding to put them in."

"I thought we were making mulled wine."

"After we hide the tokens." She dug in her skirt pocket and pulled out a few trinkets, setting them on the table. "We'll take turns. Do you want to go first? Don't forget to make a wish."

Wanting to get this over with, he grabbed the silver penny and closed his eyes momentarily—not because he was wishing for anything, but rather to pray for the strength to control his runaway emotions. He took a deep breath and opened his eyes, then shoved the penny between two strawberries.

"What did you wish for?" she asked.

Nothing, he thought, because wishing for things was pointless.

"If I tell you, it won't come true," he said aloud.

"Huh. I wouldn't have guessed you were superstitious."

"Isn't wishing on a token superstitious in the first place?"

She smiled and picked up a small ring, drawing his attention to her graceful hands. The small ring would easily fit such slim fingers. When she closed her eyes, he saw her lips move. He had no talent for lip reading, but from the way her tongue flicked behind her front teeth, he thought she'd mouthed the word "love."

Was there a man she loved? he wondered, feeling an inappropriate stab of envy, then feeling terrible for having had the feeling.

Why should it matter who she loved? He was marrying Creath.

She pushed the ring into the tart, then brought her fingers to her mouth to lick off the sticky sweet sauce that coated the strawberries. He felt his body quicken and felt ten times worse.

He was marrying Creath.

He had to remember *he was marrying Creath.*

After that, he made sure the rest went very quickly. He buried the thimble, she hid a small, boiled wishbone, and then he snatched up the last—and smallest—item.

"What on earth is this?"

"It's an anchor. To symbolize safe harbor."

"Isn't it one of those hooks for fastening clothes? It doesn't look like an anchor."

"It *resembles* one," she said defensively, as though there were any distinction. "It's symbolic, as I said. And it was the closest thing to an anchor shape I could find on short notice. Hide it, will you?"

He did, and this time he *did* make a wish. He wished to look at Chrystabel and feel nothing from now on.

When he opened his eyes, his wish failed to come true. What a shock. "Can we make the mulled wine now?"

"That's the plan. Where's the cellar?"

"This way," he said, leading her around many busy servants and down a dimly lit flight of stone stairs.

The cellar was a vaulted stone room lit with torches. The walls were lined with racks holding casks of wine and ale, and a narrow wooden worktable ran down the center of the chamber. The arched stone ceiling and thick stone walls hid the sounds of everyone bustling overhead.

"Oh, it's so quiet in here," Chrystabel said. "And so busy in the kitchen right now. Let's make the mulled wine in here."

"Let's not," Joseph said, fearing nothing good would come of being alone with her.

But she'd already left the cellar, and he found himself following. In no time at all, he was trailing her back down the steps, carrying the small cauldron full of ingredients and implements they'd collected with Mrs. Potter's help. Chrystabel carried a pitcher of boiled water.

He set the cauldron on the cellar's table and emptied it of its contents: cinnamon, nutmeg, cloves, a loaf of sugar, a grater, a long wooden spoon, a ladle, a knife, and a small roll of muslin. He'd also thrown a couple of his winter oranges and a lemon into the cauldron, thinking they might improve the flavor.

If he were being forced to make mulled wine, he might as well make it taste good.

"Do you have a decanter?" Chrystabel asked from the back of the cellar, where she'd found the casks of red wine.

He fetched one from a cupboard and began filling it from the tap. "This goes in the cauldron, yes?"

"It does." She followed him back and watched him pour. "There will be seven of us singing carols. Do you expect two decanters of wine will be enough?"

The cauldron still looked empty to him. "I think we should make it three," he said dryly. "I have a feeling some of us may drink a fair amount of wine tonight."

And he himself would be topping that list.

"And we'll also drink some during the making, for samples," she said cheerfully. "Let's use four."

"What else do we need?" he asked while going back and forth, filling and emptying the decanter. "Have we everything here?"

"Everything but brandy."

"Over there." He waved her toward the casks on the opposite wall. "You'll find another decanter in the cupboard."

She collected the brandy, poured some into the wine, grated some sugar into the cauldron, and stirred everything together. "Now we taste," she announced, lowering the ladle into the mix. "This is why I wanted help—it's always good to have a second opinion." She took a sip, then handed him the ladle. "Do you think it's a little strong?"

He sipped. "Maybe. A bit too much brandy?" He added some water. "See what you think now."

She stirred and dipped again. "Too watered down, I fear. I think we need more wine. And then we'll need more sugar."

While she grated the sugar, he fetched more wine and poured it in.

"Now it needs more brandy," she declared after tasting it again.

So it went, back and forth with tasting and adding, until the cauldron held yet another full decanter of wine, more brandy, more sugar, more water, and Joseph was beginning to feel lightheaded.

"Just a little more brandy," he said after tasting for the tenth time.

"Maybe we should add the spices before we add more brandy." She unrolled the muslin and tore off a large piece. "I'll start with four sticks of cinnamon."

"I'll slice the oranges and lemon."

"I've never heard of putting fruit in mulled wine," she said diplomatically while grating nutmeg onto the fabric.

"That's only because most people cannot get fresh fruit around Christmastime," he told her, even though he'd never heard of anyone putting fruit in mulled wine, either. "I think it will taste good." He dipped the ladle again and took a healthy swallow to evaluate. "Yes, I think it could use some fruit."

Now his head seemed to be spinning just a little. The oranges smelled delicious as he sliced them, and he moved closer to Chrysanthem—um, Chrystabel—because she smelled delicious, too. He wondered which flowers she used to make her own perfume. Did he grow all of them?

No, roses were her favorites. And he didn't have any roses.

She added a small handful of cloves to the muslin, tied up the corners, and dropped it into the cauldron.

He moved to toss in some orange slices.

She caught his free hand. "Are you sure you want to add those?"

In the cool cellar, her hand felt warm on his. Then she maneuvered her fingers to mesh with his, and *he* began to feel warm, too. He had drunk too much wine and brandy. She was close, so close he met with another heady view down the front of her bodice, which made his entire body come to attention.

Especially the lower parts.

She smelled incredible. Flowery. He loved flowers. She was vibrant like his flowers, too. Even her name reminded him of his favorite flower.

Without thinking any further—without thinking at all—he leaned in and kissed her.

He caught her little gasp in his mouth, and then she was wrapping her arms around him and moving closer. The orange slices dropped to the cellar floor as he reached to crush her to him.

The press of her strawberry-sweet lips on his set him aflame. She threaded her fingers into the long hair at the base of his neck, which made his scalp tingle. He felt her everywhere they touched, through her gown and his clothes, and he wanted to feel more.

When he parted her lips, she hesitated, as though she didn't know what to do. But then he touched his tongue gently to hers and she responded with reckless abandon, sending his blood searing through his veins. They explored each other's mouths until they were both breathless. He might have kissed her forever, but it ended when her knees began to give and he was forced to seize the table to support them both.

For a moment they just gazed at each other, speechless.

He wasn't sure why she was speechless, but he was speechless because he didn't know what to think, let alone what to say.

Kissing her had *not* felt like kissing Creath. Kissing Creath had only felt nice. Nor had kissing her felt like kissing the more experienced village girls, which had felt fun, dangerous, and daring.

Kissing Chrystabel had felt like none of those things—or maybe kissing her had felt like *all* of those things—but kissing her had also felt special, exciting, and entirely new.

Kissing her had felt *right*.

But he had to marry Creath.

"Chrysanthemum," he began—then stopped. "I mean, Chrystabel—"

"I like Chrysanthemum," she said with a tender, tentative smile. "Your favorite flower, isn't it?"

"Yes, but—"

"You can call me Chrysanthemum. I'd love for you to call me Chrysanthemum. I love you, Joseph—I've loved you since the moment I set eyes on you."

She couldn't. "But...but we just met. You cannot possibly love me. Not that I'm not lovable," he added quickly, then wanted to smack himself on the forehead. "What I meant was, you cannot love me *already*."

"I can, and I do," she said, and moved closer, and then they were kissing all over again.

She tasted divine. For a long time he just kissed her, long kisses that made his heart ache. Then he kissed a path down her throat, over her shoulders, and across the wide expanse of skin exposed in the neckline of her tantalizing, Parliament-banned gown.

His lips trailed down, just brushing the swell of each perfect breast, before he cupped her face in his hands and returned to her mouth. And when he caught her lips again with his, she felt and tasted and smelled so sweet he thought his heart might melt.

And then he thought it might break in two.

He shouldn't be doing this. But he couldn't tell her why. His head might feel woozy, but his brain still functioned well enough to know he shouldn't be kissing her, and that he couldn't tell her the truth.

He'd made a promise, and he had to keep it. He couldn't tell Chrystabel he was betrothed. He couldn't risk ruining Creath's life by revealing their plans to her or anyone else.

Wracked with guilt, he pulled himself together and broke the kiss. "I shouldn't be kissing you," he said on a gasp.

She looked disappointed and adorable, her strawberry red lips even redder from their kisses. "Why shouldn't you kiss me? You've kissed girls before. It wasn't your first kiss—I could tell."

Because it had been far from his first kiss, he felt his face heating. "It was *your* first kiss, though—*I* could tell, too."

"You could?" She bit her adorable lower lip. "Did I do it wrong?"

"You did it very, very right. But I shouldn't be kissing you."

"Why?" she repeated.

What on earth could he tell her? "I should respect you more than that. You're a proper high-born lady, and—"

"I'm not *that* proper," she interrupted. "I very much enjoyed kissing you, and I'm not-proper enough to want more kissing. I promise I won't tell anyone, if that's what has you worried."

"You won't tell anyone because I'm not going to kiss you again."

"*Why?*" she persisted.

"Because I like to think I'm a gentleman." It was the only reasonable explanation he could come up with. "And gentlemen don't kiss ladies."

"What, gentlemen only kiss harlots? You already kissed me. Why should kissing me again matter now?"

Because if he kissed her again, he might find himself unwilling to marry Creath. But he couldn't say that. So instead he said, "It matters because it's better to do the right thing late than not at all. And now I consider this subject closed."

She huffed. Adorably. "Now what?"

"Now we finish making the damned mulled wine." Grabbing more orange slices off the table to replace the ones that had fallen on the floor, he tossed them into the cauldron and used the wooden spoon to stir the mixture viciously. "Taste it," he said through gritted teeth.

SIXTEEN

"I'M SO GLAD you talked us into having a secret Christmas," Lady Trentingham told Chrystabel toward the end of their Christmas Eve supper.

So far the evening had gone even better than Chrystabel had hoped. To start, Lady Trentingham had insisted on leading a tour from room to room, exclaiming over the decorations to the point where Chrystabel had almost felt embarrassed. Halfway through the tour, Lord Trentingham had handed out goblets of wine, which had put them all in a merry mood as they'd traipsed from chamber to chamber.

Christmas spirit abounded. Everyone was dressed in their pre-Cromwell best. To complement her festive red gown, Chrystabel had added her favorites of the few jewels she owned: a small heart-shaped ruby ring, an enameled drop pendant with a single pearl, and matching single-pearl earbobs.

Joseph's deep green brocade suit made his brilliant eyes look even greener. It was trimmed with gold braid, and with his glorious long hair loose and gleaming, he looked so delicious that the sight of him made Chrystabel's mouth water. If only they could get their portrait painted, she imagined the two of them would make a perfect Christmas picture.

Arabel had found a necklace with tiny emeralds and seed pearls to wear with her green and silver gown, and Lady Trentingham was in gold again, having donned a second gold gown that was even fancier than the one she'd worn in the daytime. She wore two long strands of pearls, a beautiful cameo stomacher brooch, and amazing gem-encrusted earbobs that looked like swans. "I haven't found an excuse to wear my jewels in ages," she'd told Chrystabel. "Thank you, my dear girl!"

Creath had borrowed a lovely gown from Arabel. In white velvet with a split silver overskirt, she looked like a snow princess. Matthew couldn't seem to keep his gaze off her, which Chrystabel took as a hopeful sign. She loved helping people, and nothing would make her happier than saving Creath from Sir Leonard by helping her wed Matthew instead. Creath seemed supportive, patient, and kind—she would make a wonderful mother for Matthew's children, and Chrystabel looked forward to welcoming her as another sister.

A girl could never have enough sisters.

Excited chatter filled the dining room all the way up to the minstrel's gallery, where Chrystabel had stationed the Cartwright brothers to play Christmas tunes. Supper was nearly over, and everyone had loved the Christmas pie with its turkey, chicken, bacon, and vegetables swimming in savory gravy. The fish cooked in wine and butter, the buttered cauliflower, and the cinnamon ginger artichoke hearts had been enjoyed to the last morsel. And they had all adored Joseph's potato pudding, especially Matthew and Arabel, who, like Chrystabel, had never seen or even heard of potatoes before.

But through it all, Chrystabel had barely tasted a bite. Though she should have been exhausted after a long day of dashing about, instead she was exhilarated.

She'd finally been kissed!

And Joseph's kisses had been divine. Sublime. Everything she had dreamed of and more.

It was unfortunate that he'd decided he was too much a gentleman to continue kissing her, but she had no doubt they'd be kissing again soon. The pull between them was too great. They so clearly belonged together, it was a wonder to her that everyone around the table couldn't see it.

She couldn't wait to give him her roses tomorrow. Surely those would prompt at least a few more kisses. And after that, if he felt half as in love as she did this evening, he wouldn't countenance her leaving for Wales. Which meant the roses might also prompt a proposal.

Her heart soared at the thought.

"Chrys?" Arabel kicked her under the table. "Chrystabel, did you hear me?"

"Oh, my heavens. I'm sorry. I was daydreaming." She dragged her thoughts from the man of her dreams and looked to her sister. "What did you say?"

"Is there something you want to tell us about the strawberry tart?"

"Oh, yes, of course." While Chrystabel had been daydreaming, Mrs. Potter's giant strawberry tart had been brought in. A footman was busy cutting it. "Since we haven't any Christmas pudding, Joseph and I hid tokens in the tart. Please be careful not to swallow one, and do share what you find."

"What a wonderful idea!" Her spoon poised over the slice that had been set before her, Lady Trentingham glanced at her son and then Chrystabel. "Thank you both."

"It was Chrystabel's idea," Joseph said. "And one of the tokens is *very* small, so do take care."

"Oh!" Arabel exclaimed. "I found"—she dug something out—"a wishbone!"

Chrystabel clapped her hands. "That means you'll have luck in the coming year."

"Strawberry tart in December feels lucky enough." Arabel set the small wishbone aside. "But I suppose some luck in our new lives wouldn't be amiss. I'm hoping Wales won't feel too very different."

"People are people," Matthew said soothingly. "I'm sure we'll get on with the Welsh just fine."

If only he looked as confident as he sounded, Chrystabel might have believed him.

Lady Trentingham was the next to find a token. "A thimble!"

"A life of blessedness," Arabel told her with a smile.

The countess nodded. "Quite fitting, I suppose, since I'm blessed indeed to still have a husband and four healthy children after the war."

"And five grandchildren," Creath reminded her, making Chrystabel realize how well the girl knew Joseph's family.

"Yes, five grandchildren, too. And another on the way." Lady Trentingham seemed perfectly content this evening. "I am truly blessed."

"What is this?" Creath asked, plucking something from her tart. "A ring?"

"A sign of marriage, is it not?" Lord Trentingham looked pleased to have remembered the meaning.

Sympathy in her eyes, Arabel turned to Creath. "Not to Sir Leonard, let's hope."

"Not to Sir Leonard," Joseph said firmly.

He appeared to be gritting his teeth.

"A silver penny!" Matthew said, holding it up.

Lady Trentingham smiled. "A fortune in the offing."

"And heaven knows I could use a fortune these days." Though her brother sounded light-hearted, Chrystabel feared she knew better. "Have any pirates sailed up the Severn lately?" he added. "Perhaps we should mount a treasure hunt."

Everyone laughed except Chrystabel.

And in the end, she was the one who found the tiny anchor.

"What is *that*?" Lord Trentingham asked, squinting across the table to where she held it up.

"Half of a hook-and-eye fastener," Joseph said, sounding amused.

"It's meant to be an anchor," she protested. "Symbolizing safe harbor."

"I do wish you safe harbor, my dear," Lady Trentingham said kindly.

Safe harbor, Chrystabel thought. Ever since spotting the Dragoons, she'd seemed to be floundering.

Would Joseph be her anchor?

SEVENTEEN

*T*HE YULE LOG burned merrily in the great room, its dancing flames adding joyful ambiance to the evening. The two musical brothers were readying their instruments. Chrystabel had asked for couches and chairs to be arranged in a half circle before the immense fireplace so everyone could see one another while they sang carols after supper. Joseph was impressed. She'd thought of everything.

Impressive. Yet another *i* word.

"Mulled wine," Grosmont said before they'd even taken their seats. "We always have mulled wine on Christmas Eve. I cannot sing without mulled wine." The fellow looked to his sister. "Please tell me we're having mulled wine."

Chrystabel gave a pert little shrug. "Isn't it illegal?"

Grosmont's expression fell. "But—"

"You goose," she cut him off with a laugh, "of course we're having mulled wine! How could we celebrate illegal secret Christmas without illegal mulled wine to accompany our illegal Christmas carols? They all go together so well!"

Everyone laughed along with her.

Except Joseph. He was too busy noticing how delightful Chrystabel was. How playful. As his mother kept saying, how *refreshing*.

"I'm glad to hear it," Grosmont told her. "In this one instance only, I must commend you in your disobedient ways."

"We call that questioning convention," Mother informed him pleasantly. "*Interroga Conformationem.* Our family motto."

"Well, that's...unique." Eyebrows raised, Grosmont nodded politely. "I believe I'm in favor of questioning convention, so long as it involves drinking lots of brandy."

"Joseph and I made the mulled wine, and I fear we put in far too much brandy," Chrystabel assured him. "Just wait till you taste it." Moving closer to Joseph, she gave his arm a friendly squeeze. "He added two secret ingredients to make our mulled wine extra special."

Meeting her gaze, Joseph wondered if his face gave away his feelings. Did she know that she made his blood race with just a touch? That he couldn't stop thinking about their kisses in the cellar? Could she tell how much he wanted her?

She was beautiful and alluring, but he wanted her because of so much more than that. He wanted her because she was charming, surprising, and, yes, irresistible.

But the day after tomorrow, he was marrying Creath.

Wasn't he?

For a moment, he allowed himself to consider other possibilities. What if he didn't have to marry his friend to save her? What if his mother was right? What if they could send Creath to Wales while they helped her make a good match with another suitable gentleman?

It wasn't as though he and Creath were in love. If he got her safely married and out of Sir Leonard's reach, was that just as good as marrying her himself? Or maybe even better? Another gentleman might make her happier.

"Shall we sit?" Chrystabel prompted.

The musicians struck up a familiar tune, and everyone settled onto the couches and chairs, joining in the first verse of "Here We Come a-Wassailing." Joseph seated himself between his parents—directly across the circle from Chrystabel—and a footman offered him a steaming mug of the mulled wine. The cup warmed his hands, and the sight of Chrystabel enjoying herself warmed his heart. All the voices raised in joyous song seemed to raise his spirits, too. His chest swelled with hope and faith that everything would turn out right.

It was Christmas, after all.

And somehow, despite his earlier protests, tonight he felt lucky and grateful to be celebrating. It would have been a shame to miss this. Being here among family and friends on this magical evening was a gift, and a tradition worth fighting for.

As he sang "Love and joy come to you, and to you your wassail too," he wondered if he might have misjudged Chrystabel. Perhaps she wasn't as irrational and irresponsible as he'd thought.

"This mulled wine *is* uncommonly good," Lady Arabel said when the song ended. "You must tell us, Lord Tremayne—what are your secret ingredients?"

He couldn't help flashing Chrystabel a triumphant smile. "Lemon and orange."

"Are they imported from Spain?" Lady Arabel asked.

"I grow them in my conservatory."

"When Joseph suggested the additions, I must own I had my doubts." A gracious loser, Chrystabel inclined her head and smiled at him. "But he was right. The fruit complements the liquor and spices perfectly. Ours must be the only mulled wine with this flavor in all of history," she declared grandly.

"And it's delicious!" When Lady Arabel gulped more, she sloshed a bit down the front of her dress and giggled.

"And you weren't jesting about the brandy," Grosmont said pointedly, passing his youngest sister a handkerchief. He raised his cup to Chrystabel and Joseph. "My compliments."

"Mine, too," Mother put in. "The fruit is a brilliant innovation. How lucky I am to have such a talented son."

"And I, to have such a talented...friend," Creath finished weakly, making Joseph realize she'd been about to call him something else. Had she nearly said 'betrothed' in front of their guests? When her wide, worried eyes sought his, he sent her a reassuring smile, and she looked instantly at ease. As if, whatever happened, she trusted him to make it all right.

She always had. Three years younger than he, she'd looked up to him as an older brother and protector since they were children. When her family took ill last year, she'd run to him first and relied on him utterly. When her parents and little brother had slipped away, one by one, he'd held her as she cried and promised her he would always take care of her.

Looking at her innocent, vulnerable face now, guilt hit him like an arrow to the heart.

Puncturing all his fledging hopes and dreams and what-ifs.

Here was another what-if: What if he took an unnecessary risk with Creath's future, and she paid the price? What if he broke their betrothal for selfish reasons, and she fell into Sir Leonard's hands?

How could he have thought there might be other possibilities? There was just one possible way to ensure her safety, keep his promise, and do right by her. *Of course* anything less than that wouldn't be good enough.

Anything less was impossible.

He drained his cup of mulled wine and held it out for a refill.

"What shall we sing next?" Chrystabel asked the circle. Without waiting for an answer, she turned to the musicians. "Do you know 'Joseph Dearest, Joseph Mine?' It's my favorite."

Lady Arabel hiccuped. "Since when is it your fav—"

The music resumed, and they all began singing.

Joseph couldn't help his gaze straying to Chrystabel. Couldn't help noticing she was watching him, too. Couldn't help wondering if she'd chosen the carol for him.

> *"Joseph dearest, Joseph mine,*
> *Help me cradle my child divine..."*

Oh, how he suddenly wished he could.

He'd always liked children and knew he would have his own someday, but he'd never felt a particular *need* for them. He'd never felt fatherhood was something missing from his life. But all at once, watching Chrystabel sing sweetly, he found himself wanting to cradle her child—*their* child—more than anything.

> *"Gladly, dear one, lady mine,*
> *Help I cradle this child of thine..."*

He couldn't. He loved her, but he couldn't.
He had to tell her he couldn't.
But how could he?

EIGHTEEN

"*L*ADY CHRYSTABEL, you have outdone yourself!" The next morning, Lady Trentingham licked nutmeg and cinnamon off her lips. "A flawless Christmas Day breakfast. This panperdy could change a person's life." She speared her last bite of the panperdy, fine manchet bread fried in eggs and spices. "I wouldn't mind having you plan next year's secret Christmas."

Chrystabel wouldn't mind, either. In fact, if her dream came true today, she'd begin planning next year's secret Christmas immediately. She'd be happy to spend the rest of her life planning secret Christmases at Tremayne.

"Thank you for the kind words," she told Lady Trentingham. "I've had so much fun that none of the planning seemed like work. Shall we repair to the great room now? I have one more surprise, and then Arabel and I have a few small gifts we'd like to bestow. To be followed by Christmas Day games, of course."

"Oh, my heavens." Lady Trentingham looked alarmed. "I didn't know you were planning gifts. We normally exchange gifts on New Year's Day."

"As many families do, I know. But our family tradition is Christmas Day. I dearly hope you will accept our gifts in the spirit in which they're intended. They're very small, simply tokens of our appreciation. We're exceedingly grateful to you and your family for hosting us the past few days."

"I cannot even imagine what our Christmas would have been like on the road," Arabel put in. "Spending the holiday here has been such a pleasure."

"It's been *our* pleasure," Lady Trentingham said, rising to her feet. "If you'll excuse me for a few minutes, I shall join you in the great room forthwith."

When the rest of them entered the great room, the yule log was still burning, casting a merry glow to counteract the dull gray day outside the windows.

"Excellent job choosing the log," Chrystabel told Matthew.

"I reckon it may still be burning when we leave tomorrow," he said, sounding proud of a job well done but also somewhat dejected. When his gaze trailed to Creath, Chrystabel suspected he was already dreading saying goodbye.

That boded well. She still had most of a day to talk him into proposing to Creath. With any luck, there might be *two* betrothals before the day was out.

When Lady Trentingham joined them, taking the last remaining seat in the semicircle Chrystabel had arranged to face the great fireplace, the footmen were handing out goblets. The countess took one and sipped, then all but squealed with delight. "Warm chocolate! Such a treat!"

"My final surprise," Chrystabel said. "Mrs. Potter kindly offered her little hoard of cocoa. We used every last bean, I'm afraid."

"I cannot imagine a more fitting use for them." The countess paused for another appreciative sip. "Thank you, my dear girl. We've been leading a very quiet life since the war ended, and you've brought such joy to us. To all of us."

Was it Chrystabel's imagination, or had Lady Trentingham looked to her son when she'd said *to all of us*? Joseph's mother *did* seem to like her. Would she approve of their betrothal? Or maybe even... encourage it?

She could only hope. She thought she could come to love the countess nearly as much as she loved the countess's son. When she imagined Joseph's devoted mother becoming the mother she no longer had—barely ever had, really—she felt her heart swell with joy.

"This is for you, Lady Trentingham." Chrystabel handed her a gaily wrapped package. "From Arabel and me. We made it especially for you."

Joseph's mother pulled the end of the bow that secured the fabric, which fell open to reveal the bottle of perfume. "Oh, my heavens, thank you." She uncorked it and sniffed. "It's exquisite. Is that lavender?"

"Rosemary, actually."

"How refreshingly unexpected!" Lady Trentingham's eyes sparkled. "Somehow you figured out just what I like."

Chrystabel shrugged. "I just seem to know what fits a lady."

"For you." Arabel handed a similar package to Creath. "We hope you'll like it."

Creath held the package gingerly. "I haven't offered you hospitality."

"You've offered us friendship," Arabel said. "Go on, open it."

Still looking uncertain, Creath slowly untied the bow. As she uncorked the bottle and waved it beneath her nose, her expression of concern changed to one of delight. "Lilac?"

Chrystabel nodded. "And vanilla and a few other sweet things. Do you like it?"

"I love it. Thank you so much." Creath dabbed a little on her wrist. "I shall make it last as long as I can."

Chrystabel had to bite her tongue to keep from saying she'd make her more when she ran out. Creath wasn't matched with her brother yet.

"Lord Trentingham, this is for you." Arabel rose to hand him a square package.

"This is unnecessary—and heavy." He untied the bow, and as the fabric fell away, a smile spread on his face. "A set of books. *Dell'istoria civile del Regno di Napoli.*"

It was four volumes, bound in vellum over boards. "What does that mean?" Lady Trentingham asked.

"It's a history of the Kingdom of Naples. Written in Italian."

Arabel nodded. "Your son told me you're something of a linguist. I can read only a little bit of it myself, so we hope you'll enjoy the books more than we can."

He laughed and assured them he would. "And I'll teach you some Welsh before you leave, if you'd like."

"Oh, that would be the best Christmas gift!" Arabel all but bounced back to her seat.

She was soon off her chair again, because when she opened her gift from Chrystabel she danced around gleefully, holding the marigold gown to her front as though she were wearing it to a grand ball. Even though grand balls were forbidden now.

Arabel gave Chrystabel two beautifully decorated hair combs that had belonged to their grandmother. Their fancy scrollwork tops were inlaid with seed pearls and many tiny diamonds. "I hid them when Father took the jewels to sell," she explained.

"Since you mentioned jewels..." Lady Trentingham reached into a drawstring purse she'd brought downstairs with her. "I hope you girls will wear these in the very best of health," she said, pulling out three long, lustrous strands of pearls.

Chrystabel gasped. "We cannot accept these!"

"Of course you can," Lady Trentingham said, rising to hand a strand to her and the others to Arabel and Creath. "I still have a dozen or more strands of my own. Every young lady should own a nice strand of pearls. I wish I could see them on you next Christmas," she said almost wistfully.

If Chrystabel got her way, she would. "Thank you," she breathed as she slid the pearls over her head and settled them around her neck.

As Arabel and Creath echoed her thanks, Chrystabel smiled down at her strand. "I will treasure this always and remember how kind you were to allow me to make a secret Christmas."

It had turned out to be her best Christmas ever. Here, among strangers who had become friends, she'd proven to herself that she didn't need her mother to plan and celebrate a magical Christmas.

Suddenly knowing what to give her brother, she all but leapt off her chair.

As she walked toward him, he held up his hands defensively. "I need nothing," he said. "I have nothing for you. I had plans, but then the Dragoons arrived, and—"

"It doesn't matter," she interrupted, slipping her hand into her pocket and drawing something out. "I want to give you this."

The silver glinted in the firelight.

"Father's pendant?" Matthew's eyes widened. "He gave it to *you*, Chrys. It's yours."

Coming closer, she draped the long chain around his neck. "It's yours now. As it should be. Passed down the generations from father to son." She touched the lion one last time. "I was just keeping it for you."

Silently, she bade her father goodbye. Silently, she forgave him for leaving her. She had a new man to love now, and Arabel had been right: At nineteen, she didn't need her parents anymore. Though she'd miss her father always, she was at peace with his passing. She'd remember him every day, and she'd especially remember him every Christmas, when she honored his memory by keeping the traditions he'd loved.

The pendant looked right on Matthew, and when he tucked it beneath his shirt as their father had worn it—next to his heart—that seemed right, too. Evidently *this* tradition had more value than she'd thought.

"I have one gift left," she said, swiveling to face Joseph. "Will you come with me?"

NINETEEN

"**M**E?" **JOSEPH LOOKED** at Chrystabel's empty hands and back up to her shining eyes. "Where are we going?"

"To your conservatory." She glanced around at everyone else. "May we be excused for a few minutes? We'll be right back."

"Just the two of you?" Father frowned. "That strikes me as rather improp—"

"Oh, let them go," Mother interrupted. "She said they'll be right back. In the meantime, what game shall we start playing?"

Apparently taking that as permission, Chrystabel left the room.

Joseph followed, feeling thickheaded as he trailed her through the corridors. How did she always manage to get her way? What could she possibly have for him in his conservatory? And how on earth would he keep himself from kissing her when she gave him whatever it was?

He feared he knew the answer to the last question: He wouldn't. Though he'd awakened this morning with renewed determination, every moment in her presence seemed to chip away at his resolve. Following her, he couldn't help but notice her shapely back and the graceful sway of her hips. His fingers ached to span her slim waist.

He clenched his fists.

Today she was wearing some sort of shimmery Christmas-green fabric that set off her milk and roses complexion. The gown had another low-cut bodice that drew his attention to all the wrong places. They hadn't even reached his conservatory yet, and he wanted to rip that gown off her already.

"Here we are," she said unnecessarily when they got to the door. Uncharacteristic for her, she looked anxious. "Do you want to go inside?"

He wasn't sure he did. Which mattered not, because she didn't wait for an answer before reaching across him to undo the latch and push past him into the cavernous chamber.

He would have to remember she wasn't patient, he thought—

—then chided himself.

There was no need to remember anything about Chrystabel. Her family was leaving tomorrow, probably around the same time he'd be marrying Creath, and it was unlikely he'd ever see her again.

He still hadn't found the right way to tell her he couldn't marry her, but he had to do it anyway. Here. Now. There was no sense in putting it off any longer.

Determined to get the confession over with, he steeled himself and followed her inside. Then stopped short when he saw what awaited him in the center of the massive chamber.

Chrystabel stood beside a dozen big pots she'd evidently borrowed from his stash along the wall. Each had a dormant plant stuck inside, not planted but rather just leaning this way and that, their roots wrapped in canvas. Bright red ribbon bows were tied to a few of the thorny canes.

"Roses?" he asked on a gasp.

"Yes," she said in a nervous rush. "I brought them from Grosmont Grange. I was planning to replant them at Grosmont Castle, but I want you to have them instead. You said you don't have any roses."

For a moment he just stood there, stunned. And touched. There wasn't a more perfect gift for him in all the world. He was astonished to find she knew him so well after just three days' acquaintance.

But he couldn't take her roses.

Not when he was about to crush her heart.

"Chrystabel." He was vexed to hear his voice break. "I thank you with everything I have in me. But I cannot take your roses. They're your favorite flower. Your favorite scent." Seeing a stubborn look come into her eyes, he had a thought. "Maybe one bush, if that makes you happy, but not all of them."

"I want you to have all of them." If anything, the stubborn look only got stubborner. "I'd probably kill them anyhow—I know nothing about caring for roses, and our groundskeeper chose to stay in Wiltshire."

"I'm certain your brother will hire groundskeepers in Wales. And I don't need a Christmas gift from you, Chrysanth—Chrystabel." Holy Hades, he *had* to stop calling her that. It was only making things worse. "I don't have anything to give you in exchange, anyway."

"Yes, you do," she said in a tiny little unChrystabel-like voice.

"I do?" For the life of him, he couldn't imagine what.

An odd look came into her eyes before he saw her square her delicate jaw. "You do," she repeated more firmly. "You can give me *you*. And then you'll be able to give me roses for my perfumery. Years and years of roses."

And with that, she threw herself into his arms.

Unbidden, his own arms went around her—he was but a man, after all. A man who wanted her, and she felt heavenly and smelled better than his garden in full bloom. He was terribly moved by her generous gesture, and now he was horrified to find himself holding her—until she crushed her mouth to his. Then he wasn't moved or horrified anymore, because he was too busy being consumed.

They hadn't shared many kisses, but the rush of heat he felt seemed familiar anyway. It smacked him in the gut and spread out, and it felt *right*.

And it seemed she had learned a lot from their first kisses. Her lips parted, inviting him in, and they both sank into the caress. His remaining resolve disintegrated, no match for the force that was their overwhelming need for each other.

When he found his hands moving to detach her stomacher, he caught himself and pulled back with an almost painful effort.

What in the name of heaven, hell, and the rest of the universe was he doing?

"I'm betrothed," he choked out. "I cannot do this."

"You're *what?*"

"I'm betrothed. To Creath." Seeing shock flood her face and tears well in her eyes, he hastened to explain. "I swore to keep it a secret, but I cannot keep it secret anymore—not from you. Because no matter how much I wish I could wed you instead, I must marry Creath tomorrow to save her from Sir Leonard."

His Chrysanthemum went white. He preferred pink chrysanthemums, he thought absurdly.

"Oh," she said, looking devastated. "Oh." He saw her swallow hard, as though she had a giant lump blocking her throat. "I had no idea."

"Of course you didn't." Guilt churned in his stomach. "I'm sorry. I'm so sorry. I wanted to tell you earlier, but my parents and Creath and I—we all pledged to keep silent, for fear of the news reaching Sir Leonard. How could you have known?"

"I don't know, but I feel like I should have known somehow. Everyone tells me I'm observant—and I am. I should have figured it out." She blinked back the tears. "I should have realized when you wouldn't kiss me again in the cellar, because I knew you wanted to. Because we so clearly belong together, don't you think? I mean, don't you *know?*"

He did know—he had never felt that rush of heat with anyone besides Chrystabel, and somehow he knew he'd never find anyone else who could make him feel that heat again. But he wasn't about to admit that now. It would only make this even harder.

Instead he said as calmly as he could, "Creath is my best friend, my oldest friend. I cannot abandon her. I cannot. I gave her my word. I'm sorry."

And then she shocked the holy hell out of him by saying, "You don't need to be sorry, because I can fix this."

The color had returned to her face. Her voice had grown stronger, more confident. Apparently she was over her upset already. Devastated Chrystabel had transformed back into impulsive, impertinent, irresistible Chrystabel—the Chrystabel he'd fallen in love with—in the space of a few sentences.

The leap of hope he felt was ridiculous. "How? How do you propose to fix this unfixable thing?"

"Matthew can wed Creath tomorrow in your place. He can save her from Sir Leonard, and then you'll be free to marry me."

"What?" He couldn't have come up with a more harebrained solution if he'd tried. "What on earth makes you think your brother would agree to that?"

"He will be happy to agree to that. He as much as admitted to me that he's fallen for her, and I'm sure she cares for him, too."

Last night he'd decided she might not be irrational, but *irrational* didn't even begin to describe her plan. "Don't give me hope where there is none, please. The two of them cannot be in love. She would have told me—she tells me everything. And besides, she just met him."

"I just met you, you just met me, and—well, look how we both feel. At least, I *think* you feel like I do." Evidently his eyes gave her the answer she was looking for, because she rushed on without him saying anything. "If we could fall in love in less than three days, why can't they?"

"One day," he admitted miserably. "I cannot credit it, but I fell in love with you in one day."

He knew that now.

He'd been denying it, but there was no sense in trying to fool himself any longer.

"I fell in love with you in zero days, Joseph. The minute I saw you. There's no reason Creath and Matthew can't be in love, too. Maybe she doesn't tell you everything. Maybe you're wrong." She drew a deep breath and crossed her hands over her Christmas-green bodice, as though she were trying to hold her heart inside. "I think you're wrong. I think we need to go back to the great room, so you can talk to Creath and find out how she really feels."

"Very well," he said. He didn't hold out much hope, but her plan was his *only* hope, so he'd ask. "I'll go talk to her right now."

Chrystabel pulled him out of the conservatory so quickly, he had a hard time keeping up with her.

Back in the great room, their families were playing Hunt the Slipper. Despite his emotional turmoil, Joseph felt a tiny twinge of amusement at seeing his father on the floor playing such an undignified game. Pacing back and forth, he waited until Creath had passed the slipper before tapping her on the shoulder and beckoning her from the room.

He drew her up the grand staircase and around six times to the top floor of the castle, where they couldn't be overheard.

"Are you in love with Lord Grosmont?" he asked with no preamble.

"What?" Her eyes widened in astonishment. "What on earth gave you *that* impression?"

"Chrystabel." He blew out a breath. "She thinks you and her brother are in love, and she said you'd rather marry him than me."

"Joseph! How could you believe such a thing? I don't know Matthew at all—I just met him—and I've known you forever. Of course I wouldn't rather marry him!"

He took note of her use of the man's given name. "Are you sure?"

"Of course I'm sure. Unless..." Her gaze turned speculative. "*You* wouldn't rather I marry Matthew, would you?"

"Of course not." It struck him that they were both uttering a lot of *of courses*, which could also mean the opposite. But Creath was the most honest, straightforward person he knew. And he couldn't crush her by telling her anything but, "I want to marry you, Creath. You're my best friend, and I look forward to marrying you tomorrow."

When God didn't strike him with lightning for that lie, he figured He approved of that decision.

Which did nothing to alleviate the knot of pain that was twisting in his gut.

"Oh, my God, Joseph, look." Creath was staring out the window at the distant road, barely visible even from their lofty height. "It can't be...?"

He peered out. "What the devil? It's still two days till Saturday—"

"It's him." Creath had gone white as death. "He's early."

TWENTY

*C*HRYSTABEL PASSED the slipper beneath her skirts to Lord Trentingham, wondering what Creath was telling Joseph. She wished she were as confident in her plan as she'd led him to believe.

What if she were wrong? What if Matthew hadn't quite fallen in love with Creath yet, or what if he had but was too cautious to tie the knot quickly? When she'd mentioned marriage yesterday, he'd dismissed the notion out of hand.

Or what if Matthew loved Creath, but she didn't love him back? Creath had run away when he'd kissed her, after all. Chrystabel was fairly certain she'd seen signs of love, but this *was* her first match-making endeavor.

Or worst of all, what if Creath loved Joseph and wanted to marry him regardless of whether there was another alternative? What if she rejected Matthew's proposal and held Joseph to his promise?

She was so preoccupied with her worries that it took her a moment to react when Joseph stumbled back into the great room, closely followed by Creath.

"Sir Leonard's on his way!" he hollered. "Half a mile distant at most!"

Icy fear gripped Chrystabel's heart. Doom approaching. It felt like the Dragoons all over again.

"Why aren't you in the priest hole?" Joseph looked to Creath as if he'd just noticed she'd trailed him into the chamber. "Go get in the priest hole!"

She shook her head wildly. "I-I can't," she gasped, looking terrified. "It was *so* dark I couldn't breathe, I just—"

"I'll take a candle and go with her." Matthew jumped up from the floor and grabbed Creath's hand. "Let's go!" As he pulled her from the room, he called over his shoulder, "Someone will need to follow us and close the false bottom over our heads."

"We can't let Sir Leonard see us celebrating Christmas!" Chrystabel rushed to the fireplace and began yanking down greenery. "Where can we hide all of this?"

"Mother, Father, stay here." Joseph grabbed a couple of newsheets from a rack and tossed them to his parents. "When Sir Leonard shows up, he'll find you passing a lazy winter morning in your great room. Lady Arabel, Chrystabel, we'll collect all the trimmings and hide them in the priest hole."

Arabel rushed off. Chrystabel pulled the last of the decorations from the great room and ran through the small sitting room, down the corridor, and into the bedchamber with the priest hole. Craning her neck over her armful of greenery, she saw the wardrobe cabinet's doors were still open, the false bottom raised and still leaning against the side.

"Watch out below!" she called and tossed it all down the hole, hoping the trimmings weren't falling on Matthew and Creath.

All the while, she marveled at Joseph's ability to take charge during an emergency. He would make her an excellent husband, if only everything could work out.

When she turned around, Arabel shoved more decorations into her hands. Then Joseph showed up with yet more. "I fear Sir Leonard must be here by now," he said.

"I'll go check," Arabel said and ran off again.

When Chrystabel went to fling more wreaths and garlands into the priest hole, Joseph held her back. "They might land on the stairs and create a hazard. Let me take them down. It's safer."

"We need to gather the rest!"

"This is the last of it. And I doubt Sir Leonard is here to catch us celebrating Christmas, anyway. He wants his bride."

Below, Creath whimpered.

"I'm on my way," Joseph called to her. His arms full of greenery, he began backing down the steep wooden staircase, his gaze on Chrystabel above. "Wait till I'm down, then toss me your decorations and follow. Watch the third step—it's broken."

Chrystabel leaned into the wardrobe cabinet and glimpsed a room far below. The dim light of Matthew's candle flickered on walls made of stone. The chamber was surprisingly large for something called a priest hole, and sparsely furnished with a small wooden table, two hard chairs, and a tall, narrow bookshelf against one wall. And a bed. Well, a pallet, really—it didn't have any bedclothing. She supposed a hiding priest couldn't expect anything more comfortable.

Even with his arms full, Joseph descended the long staircase quickly. He disappeared for a moment before stepping back into her view. His hands were empty now. "I'm ready," he called softly.

Chrystabel dropped the last of the decorations into the dimness and followed, avoiding the third step.

No sooner did she reach the bottom than Arabel arrived above. "He's here! With an ancient priest-hunter, no less! He saw me, so I'm going back to pretend I'm passing the morning with Lord and Lady Trentingham." With that, she slammed the false bottom into place over their heads.

Matthew's candle blew out, leaving them in sudden darkness.

Creath whimpered again.

"Hush," Chrystabel heard Matthew whisper. "It's going to be all right. We will keep you safe."

As Arabel banged the wardrobe doors closed above, Chrystabel imagined Matthew gathering Creath into his arms. She couldn't see anything, so she didn't know whether he'd done so. But she wished she could see Joseph's reaction to Matthew comforting Creath. She was more certain than ever that her brother and Joseph's friend belonged together.

Why had she doubted herself?

She wondered what Creath had told Joseph before they'd come running back into the great room. She wished she could get him alone to ask.

"Did you hear what Arabel said?" Creath's whisper sounded panicked. "He brought a priest-hunter. A priest-hunter!"

"What's a priest-hunter?" Chrystabel asked.

"In Queen Elizabeth's time," Joseph's soft voice came disembodied through the dark, "priest-hunters—"

"He's going to find me!" Creath interrupted. "He's going to find me and make me marry him!"

"Hush," Matthew soothed again.

Someone in the priest hole moved—and a shuffling sound followed by a crash indicated whoever it was had stumbled over some decorations and fell.

"Ouch!" If it were possible to whisper a shout, Joseph had accomplished that. "Holy Hades," he hissed in evident pain. "Chrystabel, could you get the decorations off the floor and stack them all in a corner somewhere? Creath, you must calm yourself."

"He's going to find me!"

"There's a tunnel hidden behind the bookcase." Joseph sounded somewhat exasperated. "The bookcase itself is a door with a hidden latch. I'm not sure which way I'm facing now, but stand away from the walls and I'll find it."

Shuffling around in the dark in search of the trimmings she'd tossed down willy-nilly, Chrystabel bumped into the table. Now she knew where she was—at least generally. She decided to work her way around the room in a pattern, gathering the wreaths and garlands while avoiding the walls, as Joseph had asked.

"You never told me there was a tunnel from here." Creath's whisper sounded muffled, as though her face might be buried against Matthew's chest. "We used to play in here all the time, and I never knew."

"I suspect there are things you haven't told me, either," Joseph murmured a little sourly. "Ah, here it is."

Chrystabel heard a click and then the loud screech of a creaky door swinging open. She froze—as did everyone else, if she could judge by the sudden, total silence.

No footsteps sounded in the room above them.

"Creath, where are you?" Joseph called after a moment.

"Here." The single word was a terrified whisper.

"Come toward my voice. Now, listen. I'm going to get you out of here, but I don't want to talk once we leave this room, because I fear any words may echo in the tunnel and find their way out the other end. So here's what we're going to do...are you listening?"

"I'm listening."

Chrystabel was listening, too—with her heart in her throat.

She heard Joseph draw a deep breath. "We won't be able to stand up in the tunnel. We will have to crawl. I'll lead the way and you'll follow—stay close enough to touch me, all right? I want you to touch me every few moments, and if I don't feel you I'll slow down. We'll come out in the well in the well house near the stables, where no one will be able to see us emerge. The well's water level is below the tunnel exit, and there are metal rungs sunk into the well wall, like a ladder we can climb."

"Won't the priest-hunter look in the well house?" asked Creath.

"If he does, we'll hear him coming and go back down the well and into the tunnel. I'm more worried about him finding you here. This way if he finds this priest hole, you won't be here—all he'll find is the Trevors with a bunch of Christmas decorations. Do you understand everything I've told you so far?"

"I do."

"Very well. We'll stay inside the well house and keep quiet until we feel it's safe to make a run for the stables. I'll take you to Bristol and marry you, and that will be that. We no longer have any time to waste."

Chrystabel gasped as her heart plunged from her throat to her knees.

He was going to marry Creath?

Now she knew Creath's answer and wished she didn't.

"On Christmas Day?" Her heart had to be in her throat again, because she could barely force the words out. She clutched the trimmings she was holding so hard that pine needles poked into her. "You think you can wed her on Christmas Day?"

"It's officially not a holiday, remember?" Joseph sounded calm. Dead calm. Like maybe he was feeling dead inside. "All the shops are supposed to be open. All government officials have been ordered to mind their posts. Including Justices of the Peace. Yes, I think I can wed her on Christmas Day."

"But—" Chrystabel began and stopped.

"But what?" he whispered.

She didn't know what to say. So she didn't say anything. And then she realized she wasn't saying anything because there was *nothing* she could say. Nothing she could say that would stop Joseph from wedding Creath.

He'd promised to marry Creath, and he wouldn't go back on his word, because he was an honorable man.

And Chrystabel wouldn't want him any other way.

His decency was one of the many reasons she loved him.

More needles were poking into her, and the chocolate she'd enjoyed earlier was threatening to come back up.

Joseph apparently gave up waiting for her to answer. Chrystabel heard a rustling noise.

"Creath, do you feel that?" Joseph's voice still sounded dead. "It's my surcoat—have you got it? I don't want you freezing on the ride to Bristol. Put it on now. Once we make a run for the stables, we won't have time to do anything but jump on two horses. We'll need to be well gone before they realize what's happened and try to follow us."

"All right." Creath sounded petrified, but she obeyed. Chrystabel heard more rustling as she donned the surcoat. "It's too big on me."

"It will keep you warm."

"Won't you be cold?"

"Don't worry about me," Joseph said. "Are you ready?"

"I suppose so."

"Then let's go. Grosmont, close the bookcase door very slowly behind us. Hopefully that will make less noise."

"No," came Matthew's voice.

"What? You don't think it will make less noise?"

"I don't think you should go with her. *I* will go with her, and *you* can close the damned bookcase."

A stunned silence filled the dark room.

"Creath," Joseph finally whispered, "when I asked you—"

"I must *go*," she whispered back fiercely. "Before they find me. Come on, Matthew—you lead."

TWENTY-ONE

*I*N THE PITCH-BLACK, standing who-knew-how-many feet away from him, Chrystabel would swear she could *feel* Joseph's shock.

She waited for him to say something. Instead she heard him close the bookcase door very, very slowly. The protracted screech it made wasn't as loud as when he'd opened it, but it was still noisy enough that they both stood rooted in place, not daring to even breathe until it was certain they remained undiscovered.

And then he still didn't say anything for a long while.

"She wanted him to go with her," he finally whispered. "After she'd just told me she wanted to marry me. Why would she say she wanted to marry me if she wanted to marry him?"

It was doubtless a rhetorical question, but Chrystabel thought she knew the answer. "She's scared. And young. She was probably unsure of her feelings until the time came when she had to make a decision. And maybe she didn't want to risk offending her best friend." She moved toward his voice. "It appears I was right."

"It does appear so." She heard no sounds of him moving toward her, making her think he was still in shock. "I guess they're in love," he added. "I guess she'll be marrying him, after all."

Chrystabel wanted to scream with joy. But that didn't seem appropriate, as they were all still in danger. So instead she said, "I hope they won't be too cold out there," and waited to hear him whisper again so she could find him.

"I think they'll be all right," he said. "Unlike me, your brother still has his surcoat. The ride isn't too long—only twelve miles to Bristol. It's warmed up a bit, and they can stay in the tunnel if they want to keep each other warm there."

"Will you keep me warm here, Joseph? I'm scared."

She wasn't, not really—or at least not too much. How bad could it be to be found in a priest hole with Christmas decorations? They didn't hang people for that. She'd usually managed to talk her way out of tough spots in the past, and she expected that would also be the case here.

But that didn't mean she couldn't use a bit of comfort. Especially from a man like Joseph. The more she saw of him, the more she saw to love. His composure and ingenuity down here had impressed her again. He'd taken responsibility, come up with a plan quickly, and would have carried it out had Matthew not intervened. Chrystabel had no doubt he would take good care of her over the years.

He was taking a long time to answer her. "Joseph?"

"I'll be happy to keep you warm," he said at last, sounding less than happy.

Why was that? She wished she could see his face.

Moving toward his voice, she stepped forward and nearly stumbled over a chair.

"Stop," he said. "I'll come to you. I think I know where you are now."

A moment later she felt him reach out and touch her, and then he gathered her into his arms. For a long while they just stood there in the dark, holding each other. He felt warm and smelled of greenery and spicy wood smoke again—that mouthwatering scent she wanted to bottle. She wished she could stay in his arms forever.

She wanted to kiss him, but he still seemed too shocked. It seemed too soon.

"So what's a priest-hunter?" she asked softly to break the silence.

"A man who hunts priests."

She reached up to playfully hit his shoulder with a fist. "I want to know. You said something about Queen Elizabeth?"

He tightened his hold on her. "Elizabeth wanted to wipe out Catholicism, fearing she might be overthrown in favor of her Catholic cousin, Mary Queen of Scots. During her reign, it was considered high treason for a priest to even enter England, and anyone found aiding and abetting one would be severely punished. Priest-hunters were hired to find hidden priests in homes like this one."

Against her ear pressed to his shirtfront, his words seemed to rumble around in his chest. She smiled in the darkness. "What do you mean by homes like this one?"

"Homes built by wealthy Catholics. The duke who built Tremayne secretly belonged to the old church, so he planned this room to hide his priest—and their candles, crucifixes, and other Popish things—in case a priest-hunter came around. This priest hole is part of the cellars, actually. We were beside it when we made the mulled wine. But it's inaccessible from down there. The opening below the wardrobe cabinet is the only way in. Well, that and the tunnel."

His voice calmed her in the darkness. She wanted him to keep talking. "How did the priest-hunters hunt?"

"They would knock on walls to see if they were hollow, or measure the outside of the house and the rooms inside, to see if the measurements matched. They would count the windows inside and out, to see if any windows weren't included in accessible rooms. They would pull up floors and look underneath. Or they might stake out a home for days or weeks, just waiting for a Catholic priest to emerge. Sometimes priests died in the holes for lack of food and water while waiting for the priest-hunters to leave."

"That's terrible. But surely no one died here. You have the tunnel."

"I doubt a priest was ever hidden here. Tremayne's original owner was beheaded for treason before he finished building this castle. The Crown confiscated the property and eventually sold it to my great-great-grandfather. It's been ours ever since, useless priest hole and all."

"It's turned out not to be useless," Chrystabel pointed out. "Here we are in it, with a priest-hunter looking for us."

"Looking for Creath, really. But it's a wonder there are still priest-hunters around. Elizabeth's been dead for forty-eight years."

"Arabel said the priest-hunter was ancient. Perhaps she wasn't exaggerating."

"I'd guess she wasn't." She felt him tense. "Do you hear that?" he asked.

"What?"

"Someone's in the cellar next door."

Listening hard, she thought she might be hearing footsteps, barely audible through the stone wall. Then a distinct *bang*. She jumped, and Joseph's arms tightened around her.

"Is he knocking on the wall to see if there's a room on the other side?" she asked in her smallest whisper.

"Probably. But he won't be able to tell. These stone walls are too thick."

To her embarrassment, she was shaking. Her knees were threatening to give out. "Can we sit down?"

Still holding on to her, he began shuffling them toward the table.

"No," she whispered. "The bed, not the table. I want to sit beside you, not across from you."

"I don't think we should be on a bed together."

"You're sounding like your father."

"I am *not* a fust-cudgel." The words sounded like they came from between clenched teeth, and she felt him take a deep breath before he continued. "It's just that...I'm not sure I can trust myself on a bed with you."

"Why would you say that?"

"Because it's true." His whisper dropped, becoming lower, deeper. "I've never felt anything like what I feel with you, Chrysanthemum. I cannot be near you without wishing to rip your gown off."

Knowing she'd turned as red as the strawberry tart, she was glad for the darkness. She'd never heard such talk from anyone...but she wanted him to rip her gown off. She wanted that more than she would ever have thought possible.

And he hadn't even kissed her yet.

She needed to fix that.

Picturing where the bed was in her mind, she began moving them toward it. And recognized the moment he gave in. He knew the room better than she did, and he had them on that bed in a flash.

Not wanting to alarm him, she sat primly beside him and slipped her hand into his. "Are you still worried?" she asked, staring straight ahead into the blackness.

"Of course I'm still worried. Are you not?"

"Just a little." Mostly she was worrying about how to get him to kiss her. "Maybe we can help each other. What are you worrying about?"

His hand squeezed hers as he considered. "I'm worried for Creath. I'm worried your brother might not know the way to Bristol."

"We went through Bristol on our way here. You said yourself that it's just twelve miles away. I'm sure Creath knows the way, too—she's lived here since birth, has she not? Trust my brother. They will get to Bristol."

"Once they're there, he'll need to bribe a Justice of the Peace to marry them without her guardian's permission. To marry them without asking her age. I didn't tell him that."

"Matthew is clever. Besides, does Creath not know that?"

"I did mention it a few days ago."

"Then they will do fine. Trust my brother," she repeated.

She felt him shift on the bed, turning toward her. "What are *you* worried about?" he asked. "If not the two of them?"

"Your parents," she admitted.

"Really? What about them worries you?"

"What if we're found down here, Joseph, with all these holiday trimmings? Your parents could be in some trouble for breaking the law—all because I insisted on celebrating Christmas. They could lose Tremayne to confiscation, like Matthew lost Grosmont Grange. And it would be my fault."

He squeezed her hand again. "That's not going to happen. For all his bluster, Sir Leonard is a petty troublemaker. He's not going to go up against the Earl of Trentingham. At least, not over something as minor as Christmas decorations."

She did remember the earl standing up to Sir Leonard. Still... "That's not what your father said."

She felt rather than saw him wave that off. "My father can be a bit of a fust-cudgel."

When she began to laugh, he leaned forward to silence her with a kiss. Missing her lips at first, he trailed light kisses along her jaw until he found his target. The gentle caress made thoughts of laughter flee her head. But when she leaned into him, deepening the kiss, he pulled away with a regretful sigh. "Is there anything else you're worried about?"

"I don't think so."

"I thought you were going to say you're worried my parents won't approve of our betrothal."

"No!" she exclaimed in a whisper. "Your mother loves me. Although you haven't proposed, so there's no betrothal for them to approve or disapprove of, is there?"

"Holy Hades." He promptly slipped from the bed. She guessed he had gone down to a knee. He took both her hands in his, fumbling a little till he found them. "Chrystabel Trevor, will you make me the happiest man alive by agreeing to be my wife?"

"Oh, God." She wished she could see his face. But she couldn't, so she needed to touch it. She pulled her hands from his to cradle his cheeks, thrilling at the feel of his slight roughness against her palms. "Oh, God. I love you so much. Will you kiss me?"

"You haven't said yes yet."

"Yes! Dear God, yes!"

TWENTY-TWO

*S*HE'D SAID *YES*. He was going to marry Chrystabel.

Holy Hades, how would he keep his hands off her now? They'd been sitting on a bed, for heaven's sake. A *bed*.

"I love you," she whispered.

"I know," he returned, his own whisper filled with wonder. He could scarcely believe he didn't know her four days ago. "I love you, too."

"Oh, my God, Joseph—we're betrothed. We're betrothed!" Her whisper was infused with glee. She was adorable. Even when he couldn't see her, she was adorable. "You said you would kiss me if I said yes."

"I did, didn't I?" He came up off his knee and sat again beside her, turning to gather her into his arms, suddenly grateful that his surcoat was gone when he held her close. Through his thin waistcoat and his thinner lawn shirt, he fancied he could feel her heart beating. When he kissed her, she released a blissful sigh.

Keeping himself in check, he kissed her shoulder and her forehead and her throat, because that felt safer than kissing her mouth. He trailed his lips over her soft, fragrant skin. Her carefully crafted perfume assaulted his senses. For the past few days, just a whiff of that scent had sent his pulse to racing, and now he could hardly fathom that he was here all alone in a priest hole with his irresistible Chrysanthemum.

And they were betrothed.

And then, because he couldn't help himself, he went back to kissing her mouth. Her lips were simply too tempting. She felt so warm against him, and so soft, her curves melding to his body, her mouth tasting so *right*. He wished he could kiss her forever. Or at least his head wished he could kiss her forever.

Other parts were telling him that would never be enough.

"When shall we be married?" he asked, coming up for air.

"Hmm?" She sounded dazed. He felt her hand come up and search in the dark for his shoulder, then skim over to the back of his neck. Finding his nape, she curved her fingers around it and pulled his mouth back to hers, and they kissed for another long, exciting minute.

Too exciting. He couldn't take this. He broke the kiss and released her. When that wasn't enough distance, he moved apart from her and sat up straighter.

"Joseph?" she whispered. "Where did you go?" He heard her patting the bed, looking for him. When her hand found him, she crawled over and moved in back of him, kneeling on the pallet and hugging him from behind. Or at least he thought she was kneeling on the pallet— he wished he could see her. "Come back," she whispered, trying to pull him down on the bed with her. "I'm not finished kissing you."

"When shall we be married?" he asked again. "Tomorrow?"

Their wedding couldn't come soon enough for him. He couldn't wait to get his hands on her with a clear conscience.

"Not tomorrow." Wafting from behind him, her sigh felt warm by his ear. "I want a church wedding. We'll have to wait three Sundays for the banns to be called."

"Three Sundays? Three weeks? Wait, that's more than three weeks, isn't it?" It seemed a lifetime. "I want to be wed tomorrow. Church weddings aren't legal anymore, anyway."

"They're not *illegal*, either. They're allowed—they just don't count as far as the government is concerned. We can be wed by a Justice of the Peace in the morning to satisfy the law and then have a church wedding in the afternoon. Our marriage won't feel real to me if it's not blessed by the church."

"Very well," he grumbled. He certainly wanted her to feel really married.

But more than three weeks seemed a long, long time.

Not a lifetime—a lifetime and a half.

Catching him off guard, she grabbed him tighter and managed to pull him down beside her. "Can we kiss again now?" she asked.

He quietly laughed and kissed her again. And kissed her and kissed her, until he realized he was now lying half on top of her, which was not a good idea. He wasn't a fust-cudgel like his father, but he knew right from wrong. With a wistful sigh, he broke the kiss and pulled her upright again.

Chrystabel's little sound of frustrated disappointment matched his own feelings all too well. He reached out to hold her, but she broke free. He felt her moving beside him.

"What are you doing?" he asked.

"Taking off my shoes." He heard two soft *thumps* as they hit the floor. "It feels wrong to lie in bed wearing shoes."

"We're not *in* bed, we're *on* a bed." He was thankful for that. "And it's not even a bed, really."

It wasn't comfortable—it was just a thin, straw-filled pallet on top of a low wooden box that someone had probably built in the last century. Which was just as well, because God only knew how far he'd be tempted to take things on a real bed.

He heard some rustling. "What are you doing now?"

"Removing my garters, so I can take off my stockings."

"I'm not sure you should do that."

"Why not? Do you usually wear shoes and stockings in bed?"

"I told you, it's not a bed." The little rustling sounds continued. Mentally picturing her removing her garters, he swallowed hard.

"You're not going to take anything else off after the stockings, are you?"

"No," she said quickly. "Of course not."

"Good."

"Well..." She paused so long he began wondering what was happening in her head. "Do you want me to take off more?"

Oh, he wanted her to, all right.

"No," he said, and then, "yes, but no." He forced a whispery laugh. "I fear we shouldn't be alone like this."

"Perhaps not." She shifted, and he felt as if she were looking at him in the dark, evaluating his mood, his intentions. Which was impossible, of course. It was pitch-black. "But I'm glad for it," she added in a breathy whisper. "I like being alone like this."

Joseph was finding it hard to breathe.

He knew she was innocent—he'd been the first man to kiss her, for heaven's sake. But did she have to be so innocently seductive? How was he supposed to resist her when she was shucking clothing left and right?

He felt movement beside him and figured she was rolling down her stockings. Picturing *that* wasn't helping his breathing any.

"Oh, that feels so much better." He could hear the smile in her voice and imagined her wiggling her toes. He'd never seen her toes, and he couldn't see them now, but he envisioned them all pink and pretty and stopped breathing altogether.

"Let me help you with your shoes," she whispered.

Not sure he could stand her help, he leaned over and tugged them off before she had a chance. His stockings followed. He finally blew out a breath.

Her soft chuckle made him wonder if she knew what she was doing to him.

Maybe she wasn't as innocent as he'd thought.

When he straightened again, she leaned close and managed to find his lips with hers. Her mouth was so sweet, it took all he had to keep from tearing her gown off then and there. He was tired of fighting with himself. Forgetting that they shouldn't be lying horizontal together, he found himself drawing her down to the pallet again.

Or maybe she drew him down. He wasn't sure.

And lost in the moment, in the pleasure of her mouth on his, he didn't care.

TWENTY-THREE

CHRYSTABEL COULDN'T believe she was in bed with the love of her life.

Well, *on* a bed, as he kept pointing out. And the bed wasn't really a bed. Regardless, it was the most exciting thing that had ever happened to her.

Joseph was softly kissing her. One of his fingertips had found the bare skin at the base of her neck and was tracing a pattern there, sending tendrils of sensation everywhere. Exhilaration thrummed through her, making her feel warm all over.

Actually, *warm* was a weak word for what she was feeling. She burned for more.

She burned for everything.

It had all happened so fast. In mere days she'd gone from not knowing him to wanting him to learning he belonged to another, and now, miraculously, he was hers. Now she wanted him in a different way, with a fierceness she'd never even imagined.

More than three weeks. It seemed like forever. She pressed closer, parting her lips, trying to coax him into more than these soft, dreamy kisses.

Joseph pulled back. His fingers on the nape of her neck stopped moving. "Oh, Chrysanthemum," he whispered, but the whisper sounded more like a groan. She worried for a moment that he was upset and wondered why—but he didn't push her away. Instead he just waited a moment.

Their breathing sounded loud in the darkness.

Then, quite suddenly, his hand curved around the nape of her neck and brought her mouth to his again.

The lips that had been soft and gentle earlier were urgent now, more fervent. He kissed her until she felt breathless, senseless, then his mouth trailed down to play in the sensitive hollow of her throat.

His lips felt so good against her skin. His tongue drew warm circles on her flesh, moving lower, delving closer to the cleavage revealed by the low neckline of her Christmas Day gown. Her heart raced faster as new sensations rippled through her, not only where his mouth teased her, but other places, too. An ache was building inside her, a most strange and wondrous feeling.

Wishing to make him feel the same way, she reached to unknot his cravat.

He lifted his head. "You cannot do that," he murmured.

"I want to do to you the same things you're doing to me." The lace-edged fabric came untied, and she began drawing it from his neck. "This is covering places I want to kiss you. I want to make you feel—"

"You *cannot.*"

She stopped, stunned by the vehemence of his whisper. "Why?" she breathed.

"Because if you do," he said very slowly, "I fear I may not be able to keep from doing more."

Oh, was that his only problem?

Knowing he couldn't see her, she smiled as she pulled the cravat free.

"Chrysanth—"

"Joseph." Her mouth feeling suddenly dry, she licked her lips. Her heart pounded so loudly she feared he could hear it. "I want you."

"You're going to have me," he said, his whisper sounding painfully forced. "We're going to have each other. In three weeks."

"It's going to be *more* than three weeks, and I want you *now*." As her fingers went to loosen the lacing at the top of his shirt, she realized she'd never felt like this before—like a wanton, truth be told. But then, she'd never before been in love.

She opened the placket of his shirt and put her mouth to his skin as he had to hers, tasting him, faintly salty and spicy, a heady flavor that was his alone. He smelled better than any perfume she could possibly create.

She heard him swallow hard. "Your parents would not approve of this."

She kissed his neck and felt a tremor run through him. "My father is dead and my mother might as well be."

"Your brother, then."

"I care not what my brother thinks." She kissed the top of his chest in the unlaced opening, then moved up to kiss his mouth.

"You're truly bent on seducing me, aren't you?" Sounding incredulous, he allowed a light kiss, but no more. "*My* parents wouldn't like this, either."

"Your mother might."

"What? What do you mean by that?"

"What did your mother say your family motto was last night?"

She heard him sigh. "*Interroga Conformationem.* Question Convention."

"Exactly. This isn't conventional, but I think she might be all right with it."

He was silent for a long moment, while she heard and felt his breathing getting rougher. "Well, she wouldn't like *this*," he finally said, yanking her against him and kissing her again, harder than ever before.

She was shocked for a bare moment but then let herself slide into the demanding caress. He plundered her mouth, tasting of warm chocolate and Joseph. When at last he let her go, she found herself trembling with uncontrolled desire.

"Your mother likes me," she informed him shakily. "Your parents are going to be happy we're betrothed. So why can't we question convention? We're going to be married anyway, so why should we have to wait? We'll be wed in a few weeks, but I want you now."

"If you say that enough times, I might begin to believe you."

He'd made it sound like a threat. "How many more times?" she wondered. "A dozen? I want you now, I want you now, I want—"

He silenced her with another kiss, a kiss so fierce she wondered if perhaps he'd given in.

But then he drew back and was silent again.

It was a different kind of silence. She couldn't see him, but she could tell. He was fighting with himself, she was sure of it.

"I cannot do this," he said at last, his whisper sounding forced. "Not before we're married. It wouldn't be right."

"Are you a virgin, then?" she whispered.

She thought she heard him choke. "My impulsive, impertinent Chrystabel. Is there no question you're unwilling to ask?"

"No," she said shortly. "Are you one, then? Have you never..."

"I have," he admitted on a sigh.

She'd known that, of course, because he wasn't at all nervous like she was. Unlike her, he knew exactly what he was doing in—*on*—this bed. His hesitance had nothing to do with a lack of confidence and everything to do with a moral dilemma.

His answer hadn't surprised her.

"Thank you for answering my question honestly," she told him.

"But those other times were different."

He'd whispered that so softly she'd barely heard him.

"Let me guess," she returned dryly. "Because she wasn't a lady?"

"None of them were ladies."

None of them? *Them?*

Now he'd surprised her.

"How many—"

"Oh, Chrysanthemum," he interrupted, "none of them mattered. None of them made me feel anything like you do. Not anywhere even close. Forget them. Just forget them, please. Don't make me sorry I was honest."

She was still catching her breath. It took her a moment to respond, a moment to absorb the fact that she was far from his first.

"Are you done with them?" she finally asked in a tiny whisper.

"I'm done with them." He sounded desperate, but also desperately truthful. "I was done with the last one before I met you. Weeks before I met you. I am so, so done with them—"

"They why aren't you willing to bed me?" she burst out.

"Because—"

"Oh, I don't want to hear it," she cried, cutting him off. "You're a hypocrite, do you know that? I'm no better than those other girls. You and I are going to marry, so what does it matter? You're not a virgin, and I don't want to be one anymore. Please, Joseph, put me out of my misery."

"What?" He sounded completely nonplussed. "What misery?"

"The anticipation is killing me." If he could be honest, then so could she. "Martha and Cecily—my older sisters, my married sisters— both told me the first time would hurt. I want to get that over with. I want to come to you on our wedding night free of this worry. After saying our vows, I want to come to you with no reservations. I want to come to you with only joy."

He was silent for so long, she began to wonder if he'd fallen asleep.

Then slowly his fingers moved to unfasten her stomacher.

Her heart soared. She'd won.

She wanted this. She burned for him. And she truly *did* want her first time to be over and done.

"Are you certain?" he asked, his whisper low and earnest, his fingers fumbling on the stomacher's tabs in the darkness. His hands fell away. "I'm undressing you, and you're not stopping me."

"Yes, I'm certain. I'm not stopping you." She found his hands and brought them back to the stiff, embroidered garment. "I'm not."

His hands didn't move, just rested lightly against her front. Her pulse skittered. Beneath his fingertips, her breasts felt firm and overly sensitive.

A silence stretched between them. When he spoke again, his voice was even lower, more serious. "You do know what you're asking?"

She began to nod, then stopped since he couldn't see her. "I know exactly what I'm asking. I want you to make me yours. I want you to rip my gown off," she clarified, echoing his words from earlier.

Immediately, he made a little sound of capitulation.

The next thing she knew, she found herself locked in his arms, and he had his lips pressed tightly to her forehead in a caress so cherishing it made her heart twist painfully in her chest.

After a minute he pulled back, and his fingers returned to her stomacher, less tentative this time.

Her own fingers fluttered up to unbutton his waistcoat. The stiff stomacher made a soft *plop* as he dropped it to the stone floor. She pushed his waistcoat back over his shoulders and off of him, then dropped it to the floor as well.

She really had won, she thought, her breath catching in her throat.

Beneath where the stomacher had been, Chrystabel was laced tightly into her bodice. Joseph untied the bow, then went to work on the laces. "You're sure?"

Why was he still asking? Hadn't she made herself clear? Hadn't she, a rather bold girl, been bolder than ever before?

"I'm sure," she breathed. She couldn't let him back down now.

Remembering her sisters' warning, she was nervous. But feeling Joseph's hands on her, she was also excited. And the excitement overwhelmed her worry.

Every single bit of it.

Suddenly feeling frantic, she reached out to free his voluminous shirt from where it was tucked into his breeches. All she wanted, it seemed, was to feel his skin against her own. He seemed covered with so much fabric. Yards and yards of frothy fabric, all standing in her way.

With a pained chuckle he pushed her hands away. When he seemed to be struggling on the bed, it took her a moment to realize he was drawing the shirt off over his head. She imagined all of his warm, tempting skin being revealed and wished mightily that she could see it.

She couldn't. But she could touch him. She reached out, running her hands up his bare chest, feeling the taut skin and the muscles underneath.

It wasn't enough. With a tiny moan of pleasure, she shifted toward him and spread her bodice wide. A soft gasp escaped his lips as she pressed herself against him, the gossamer material of her chemise the only barrier between them.

He felt so good. Her heart beat faster. Her breathing became strangely uneven.

"Now?" she whispered.

"Not yet," Joseph said, pulling away from her a little. His fingers brushed a breast through the thin fabric of her chemise, and she felt the peak tighten into hard tenderness. Her body arched toward him involuntarily, her breath becoming even more ragged.

"Oh, Chrysanthemum," he breathed. "I cannot wait. Can you wait?"

"I cannot wait," she echoed in a whisper. "Now?"

"Not yet."

Pulling away from her again, he wrestled the heavy bulk of her double-skirted gown over her head. It joined the rest of their clothes on the floor, leaving her clad in only the chemise. She lay there, shivering, not with cold but with anticipation.

"I wish I could see you," he whispered.

"Feel me," she invited instead.

And he did. She held her breath while, with whisper-soft caresses, his hands skimmed leisurely over her middle, then traced the curve of her hip. He brushed her mouth with his as his fingers teased lightly through the fabric, then more firmly, tracing the crease where her thighs met.

A heat spread from his hand, bathing her in warmth. She moaned softly and felt Joseph smile against her lips. Before she knew what was happening, he'd tugged down her chemise and fastened his hot mouth on her bare breast, suckling gently, stroking his textured tongue over the sensitive peak.

She'd imagined kissing and mating, but she'd never imagined anything like this. Good heavens, it was indescribable. He wandered to her other breast, his mouth hot there while the air cooled the wetness he'd left behind. Driven to distraction with new sensations, she writhed against him. Her breath came in short gasps; her hands roamed the hard planes of his back. She was acting wantonly again, but she couldn't seem to help herself.

She didn't *want* to help herself.

And while she was pondering the wonder of it all, he swept off her chemise.

Leaving her bare.

She'd sometimes wondered if she might feel shy or embarrassed in this moment, but in the darkness she felt gloriously free. She pressed against him once more, feeling the ache inside her spread.

"Now?" she whispered again.

"Not yet."

"Oh, my God, *when?*" she gasped, and he caught that gasp in his mouth, reclaiming her lips in a devouring caress. While she was distracted by that, he slipped his hand between her legs and parted them gently, his fingertips trailing sensuously on her inner thighs. She began to tremble. When he brushed against the curls that guarded her most secret self, she gasped again, this time in shock and fascination.

"Hush," he whispered into her open mouth. Distracting her once more with a long, deep kiss, he slipped a finger inside her tight passageway.

Chrystabel could scarcely believe a man was touching her there, let alone moving his finger in and out of her, as he was slowly doing now. But everything with Joseph felt right. He found an exquisite spot, and waves of passion swept through her. She clutched him tighter, feeling as though her heart might burst if something, she wasn't sure what, didn't happen soon.

Then suddenly his hands left her, and she was aware of a flurry of movement. When he reached again to pull her close, she found he'd removed the rest of his clothes. His arms went around her, and they met, skin to skin, from their shoulders to their toes.

This, she thought, *is bliss.*

Down low she could feel a hardness, a hardness that made her blood race, a hardness that told her he wanted her as much as she craved him.

Her married sisters had told her about this, too.

"Now," she breathed.

"Not yet, my love." He kissed her quickly, wildly, then bent his head to trail his lips down her throat. A hot stab of lust lanced through her. And love. It was all mixed up together in her head, in her heart, in her body so aware she felt if Joseph just kissed her one more time she'd explode.

All at once she felt the sensations were more than she could bear.

"Now, Joseph. Now."

He chuckled against her, sending low vibrations through her. "Slower is better, my love. We've a long way to go before—"

"*Now.*"

His mouth left her. "Don't you like this?"

"I like it too much." She couldn't catch her breath, and her entire body sang with an awareness she'd never even imagined. "Please, Joseph, join with me now."

Everything he was doing felt good, but she wanted it all and she wanted it now. She wanted it done. She wanted this first time over with.

She couldn't stand a moment more of this sweet torture.

"Please."

She held her breath, waiting while she felt him swallow hard. "Chrysanthemum—"

"*Please.*"

He hesitated. "If you're sure."

"I'm sure!"

"Hush. You need to keep quiet, my love. You don't want to be caught down here, do you?"

Oh, God. She could think of nothing more embarrassing. She briefly considered calling the whole thing off, but he was kissing her again, softly, and then he began to move over her, apparently having given in.

Chrystabel's heart pounded, excitement blending with the fear.

She forgot about calling anything off. Instinctively she raised her knees. Seeming to support himself on his elbows, Joseph took her face in both hands and kissed her while he eased his way between her legs.

He settled against her, fitting there as if they were made to go together. An incredible urgency radiated from where his body was poised to enter hers. Her blood pumped faster.

He broke the kiss and froze.

"I cannot do this," he gritted out in a fierce whisper. "I cannot do this before we're wed."

"Oh, I believe you can," she murmured with a secret smile he couldn't see. And deliberately she raised her hips, welcoming him into her and at the same time bracing for the pain.

It wasn't as bad as she'd anticipated, but she might have cried out if Joseph hadn't covered her mouth with his. Holding her face, he stayed still and whispered senseless endearments, raining little kisses all over her cheeks.

"I'm sorry," he murmured.

But the pain was fading already, rapidly becoming an ache of another kind...an ache so exquisite she found herself straining against him in hope of easing it.

He kissed her mouth, and then he moved in her.

A gasp of wonder escaped her lips.

"Now," he whispered.

She couldn't seem to form as much as a single word.

He moved in her again, and then they moved as one in a dance as old as time, a dance far more intimate than the scandalous volta. Slowly and then faster, the feelings building to a crescendo, higher and higher until Chrystabel couldn't quite hold back a scream.

Joseph placed a hand over her mouth as she erupted in pleasure so intense she was half convinced she was flying. Up and up, flying higher yet when she felt him go with her. Her own hands went everywhere, trying to feel him all at once as her breath came in long, shuddering sighs, matched by his.

It seemed a long time later when she drifted back down to earth. Joseph was still pressed close, his heart beating in a cadence to match hers. For the next few minutes, she just lay beside him, content to listen to the two of them breathing while she savored the new and wonderful sensation of his warm body against hers.

"It was bliss," she whispered when she finally felt able to form words.

"It was." He kissed her cheek, her nose, her forehead.

"It was beautiful."

"It was." He kissed her mouth.

Her lips clung to his for a long, satisfying moment. "I'm so glad I talked you into doing this *now*."

"So am I." She heard a smile in his voice. "Now you'll come to me on our wedding night with only joy."

"Oh, yes, it was joyful." She felt deliciously worn out. "And our wedding is three weeks away. *More* than three weeks away. By the time of our wedding night, I reckon we'll have had plenty of practice, so that everything will be very, very joyful."

"What?" She felt him pull away a little. She couldn't see him, but she sensed he was looking at her with a bit of consternation. Or trying to look at her, anyway. "We'll be in my parents' home all of those three weeks. At least"—she heard his breath catch—"I assume we'll both be in my parents' home. You're not still planning to go to Wales, are you?"

"Of course not," she said with a soft laugh.

She'd never expected to laugh in bed with a man, but it felt right.

Everything with Joseph felt right.

"I never wanted to go to Wales at all," she added, shifting closer. "But we'll be in your parents' home *after* those three weeks as well, won't we? This is Tremayne, and you're the Viscount Tremayne."

I'm going to be the Viscountess Tremayne, she thought, feeling a little thrill run through her. *I'm going to be Lady Tremayne.*

"Yes, we'll be here at Tremayne afterwards too. But we'll be married then. We cannot 'practice' in my parents' home before we're wed. Surely you understand that."

"Surely I don't." He was absolutely darling. "We're in your parents' home now, aren't we?"

"They cannot find us here!" he exclaimed too loudly. "We're in a priest hole!"

"Hush!" she admonished in a whisper. "You need to keep quiet, my love. You don't want to be caught down here, do you?"

She thought she heard him choking, but then she realized she was hearing suppressed laughter. "That's the second time within an hour that you've parroted my words," he said once he got himself under control. "Shall I assume you'll be doing this all of my life?"

"All of *our* lives. And I'm afraid so." It actually wasn't much a habit of hers, but she'd look for opportunities since it amused him. "I hope you'll still want to marry me anyway."

"Of course I still want to marry you. But I don't want to do this again until we're married." She heard a little pout in his voice. "Not in my parents' home."

"Really? Really, Joseph?" She pressed closer, feeling evidence that he was lying. "I think you *do* want to do this again. But you just go on thinking that."

"I know what *you're* thinking," he accused. "I can tell from your tone that you're thinking you'll seduce me again. Well, I have more control than you think. It won't work. You won't be able to seduce me until you have a wedding ring on your finger."

"You think not?" she said, wishing she could send him her best challenging look.

But it was pitch-black.

So she just whispered, "Watch me."

TWENTY-FOUR

*C*HRYSTABEL AND JOSEPH had lain wrapped in each other's arms for a long while, sometimes kissing and sometimes just breathing. Then they'd risen and dressed, laughing softly as they felt around for their clothes on the floor. After that, exhausted, they had crawled back on the bed to rest, chatting in whispers while they waited for Arabel to return and tell them it was safe to come out. At some point they had fallen asleep.

Chrystabel woke when she heard a scraping sound overhead.

The wardrobe's false bottom was being removed. For a moment, she panicked—her heart began beating double-time. But then she blinked herself more wakeful and chided herself, because surely it was just Arabel, coming to free them at last.

When the bottom was lifted, dim light filtered in first.

"Arabel?" she called softly.

Bright light flooded the chamber as a torch was thrust into the opening above. "I knew it!" Sir Leonard crowed as he descended, sounding disgustingly pleased with himself.

Chrystabel and Joseph bolted upright simultaneously.

She heard the third step snap, a loud *crack* like a cricket bat slamming a ball in the Grange's village square. But Sir Leonard didn't falter. He came closer, waving the torch before him in victory.

"I knew I'd find you hiding with this foul lot. Mark my words, girl, your great friend Trentingham will finally get what's coming to him. And as for you, Creath—you will marry me *today*, or—"

"Who is Beth?" Chrystabel squeaked.

"Who is...? Who the devil are *you*?" he roared as he reached the bottom.

Apparently Joseph hadn't completely reattached Chrystabel's stomacher in the dark. Working the remaining tabs as surreptitiously as possible, she shakily rose. "I'm Lady Chrystabel Trevor," she said with all the dignity she could muster—which was quite a bit. "Don't you remember me from when you came by on Tuesday evening? I'm a guest of the Ashcrofts. I don't know who this Beth is you're speaking of, but I can assure you she's not here."

"Not Beth, you halfwit—Creath! It rhymes with *breath*!" He crisscrossed the room frantically, poking the torch into every corner in a fruitless search for his betrothed.

"Creath isn't here, Sir Leonard," Joseph growled, knotting his cravat from his seat on the bed. "It's the second time you've made this mistake. If you leave now, perhaps we'll pretend it was an honest one."

"Do you take me for an idiot, boy? If you're not harboring my bride, why the hell are you hiding in a priest hole?" he bellowed furiously, pulling a pistol from his wide boot top and brandishing it at Chrystabel.

Her heart jumped into her throat. She shrank back, falling onto the bed at the same time Joseph leapt up and shoved Sir Leonard hard in the chest with the heels of both of his hands.

Sir Leonard stumbled back.

"Leave her alone!" Joseph hollered. "You don't point guns at ladies! And we're down here because we have Christmas decorations, you witless worm! That's right—you caught us celebrating Christmas," he sneered. "What are you going to do about it? Are you going to turn us in, Sir Justice of the Peace? Or are you going to shoot us? Is this what your life has come to, harassing neighbors for celebrating holidays?"

"Damn right I'm going to turn you in! Right after I find Creath!" Following one last look around that failed to reveal her, Sir Leonard turned on a heel and stormed back up the steep staircase, his torch in one hand and the pistol still in the other.

Joseph rushed up the stairs after him. "Wait! The third step!"

Sir Leonard half-turned, but it was too late.

One leg crashed through the ruined step. Terror flashed in his eyes. His pistol went off. As the bullet hit the wall behind her, Chrystabel screamed and saw the rest of him plunge through the staircase.

With a great *thump*, he landed on his back, followed by a hideous *crack* as his head hit the rock-hard ground. He lay there half behind the staircase, his neck at an odd angle, his arms spread out to the sides. The torch guttered against the stone floor, plunging the room back into darkness except for a sliver of dim light that filtered in from the opening above.

It took a few seconds for Chrystabel to find her voice.

"Oh, my God, Joseph! Oh, my God! I think he's dead!"

"What? Did you say something?" Still halfway up the stairs, Joseph shook his head. "I can't hear you. Did you say something?"

"I *yelled* something!" She was yelling now as she rushed toward him. "I said Sir Leonard is dead! What's wrong with you?"

"My ears are ringing. They hurt." He shook his head again, then clapped his hands over his ears with a grimace. "They feel all clogged up."

She gasped when his fingers came away coated in blood. "Joseph!"

"The gun went off right by my head, Chrysanthemum, and now I cannot hear you!"

TWENTY-FIVE

A month later

$\mathcal{T}$HE CHURCH OF St. Mary the Virgin was immediately adjacent to Tremayne Castle. A high, covered timber bridge linked the two buildings. The duke who built Tremayne had used the bridge to directly reach a church balcony that overlooked the sanctuary, so he could come and go and attend services without deigning to speak to any parishioners.

The duke didn't sound like a nice man. Chrystabel thought maybe he'd deserved his beheading.

In any case, the bridge was long in disrepair, so the Ashcrofts and Trevors had walked out to the road and over to the church for the wedding on this fine, if cold, day. Since big church weddings were frowned upon by the Commonwealth government, there were only the seven of them attending and no parishioners to talk to, anyway.

As they weren't really out in public, Chrystabel had decided to wear her new strand of pearls for her church wedding, together with a pre-Cromwell gown: a pale blue confection with silver scrollwork and seed pearls on the stomacher and underskirt. Joseph had gaped appreciatively when he saw she'd changed into it after this morning's civil ceremony. Although they had already been declared man and wife by a Justice of the Peace, she didn't feel married yet. She thought she might not feel married until after the wedding breakfast. She'd been planning the menu for weeks.

But this church service was taking so long that she feared half of the delicious meal might spoil before their families got to enjoy it.

The tall, majestic church had been built in stages over the last several centuries. It had a Norman doorway, a Gothic chancel, a Tudor bell tower, a soaring dark wood hammerbeam ceiling, and many beautiful, colorful stained glass windows. Standing before the intricately carved altar while the vicar read the interminable service, Chrystabel felt dwarfed in the enormous old building. But she couldn't help smiling at the thought that she was getting married in the Church of St. Mary the Virgin when she wasn't a virgin.

She was very much not a virgin now.

Down in the priest hole, when she'd told Joseph that his mother might be all right with them making love before marriage, she hadn't really believed that. She'd just been trying to talk him into bedding her. But now she had to wonder, because either Lady Trentingham *did* question convention to that extent, or else the woman was completely oblivious.

Chrystabel had only had to seduce Joseph *once*.

After that, *he'd* taken over the seducing.

In the weeks since their betrothal, Joseph had made love to Chrystabel in his conservatory. He'd made love to Chrystabel in his bedchamber. He'd made love to her in her bedchamber, in the great room, in the library, and once in the kitchen when they'd sneaked down in the wee hours for a midnight snack.

That had ended up being a different kind of snack than the one Chrystabel had originally had in mind. A much better one.

It seemed they couldn't keep their hands off each other. He was constantly surprising her, teaching her new and different ways to enjoy each other. Though at first she'd found herself wondering where he might have learned all the different ways, she was far too busy feeling blissful to bother herself about that—so she'd decided he was just an inventive lover. When she envisioned their future, full of exciting days and even more exciting nights, she felt like the luckiest woman in the world.

And she had a secret: She'd missed her monthly two weeks ago. She'd been waiting for their wedding night to tell Joseph, as a wedding present. She hoped he'd be as happy as she was—she couldn't wait to hold their babe in her arms. And she knew she'd be a much better mother than her own mother. She felt it with a certainty that filled her with peace and gratitude. On the brink of motherhood herself, she knew she'd finally forgiven Mother in her heart.

After all, she'd learned how *not* to be a mother from her, and that was a priceless lesson.

Besides, she had a new mother now, a kind and nurturing one. This morning, when Lady Trentingham had requested she call her 'Mother' from now on, Chrystabel had felt a warm glow from the top of her head to the tips of her toes.

After droning on for another twenty minutes, the vicar turned a page in his prayerbook and cleared his throat.

At last, Chrystabel thought. Her heart soaring, she squeezed Joseph's hand as the vicar began chanting their vows.

"Joseph Ashcroft, The Right Honorable Viscount Tremayne, wilt thou have this woman to thy wedded wife, to live together after God's ordinance in the holy estate of matrimony?" He was a very soft-spoken man, which she found a bit worrisome. "Wilt thou love her, comfort her, honor, and keep her in sickness and in health; and, forsaking all others, keep thee only unto her, so long as ye both shall live?"

An expectant silence filled the church.

"Say that last part louder," Chrystabel whispered.

"So long as ye both shall live?" the vicar repeated.

"Louder."

"So long as ye both shall live?" he fairly yelled.

"I will," Joseph said, his confident words finally booming through the magnificent arched sanctuary.

Along with everyone else, Chrystabel breathed a sigh of relief.

She'd recovered quickly from the shock and horror of seeing a man die—Sir Leonard had been a bad man, after all. But Joseph still hadn't fully recovered his hearing. Chrystabel thought his ears would eventually heal, but over the last weeks she had assured him—very loudly and very often—that she would be just as thrilled to wed him hearing or deaf.

The soft-spoken vicar cleared his throat again and looked back down at his *Book of Common Prayer*. "Lady Chrystabel Trevor, wilt thou have this man to thy wedded husband..."

Off to one side, Chrystabel's brother and his new wife held hands, whispering their own vows surreptitiously. They hadn't been able to have a church wedding, so it warmed her heart to see them pretending to have one today.

After their civil ceremony, they'd returned from Bristol toward the end of Christmas Day and been thunderstruck to find Sir Leonard dead.

"Do you want our marriage annulled?" Matthew had asked Creath solicitously. "It hasn't been consummated yet, and now your odious cousin cannot come after you..."

Creath had burst into tears. Racking, heart-rending, inconsolable tears.

"You're an idiot!" Chrystabel had railed at her brother.

"I'm inclined to agree," Arabel had put in politely.

At Creath's demand, their marriage had been consummated within the hour. Now they were living in her father's mansion while they built a new house on her land. Given that it had taken nearly a year for the authorities to find and verify Sir Leonard as her father's heir, they figured they had at least that much time before the next baronet came to claim Moore Manor.

Creath's son wouldn't inherit her father's title, but eventually he'd inherit Matthew's title instead. He'd be an earl instead of a baronet. She was fine with that.

Matthew made no secret of the fact that he was glad he hadn't needed to move to Wales with his sisters. He also no longer had financial troubles, since his income from Grosmont in Wales plus Creath's income from her own lands here had them well on their way to rebuilding the Trevor family fortune.

But that was not why he had married Creath, of course. Anyone could see that he loved her.

If she had agreed to the annulment, he would have been devastated.

Arabel and Creath had become great friends, a convenient turn of events since they were now sharing a home. Arabel would naturally continue living under her brother's roof until she found a husband. Or rather, until her matchmaking sister found a husband for her. At seventeen, Arabel was still in no hurry to wed, although, thanks to Chrystabel's bliss and reassurance, she'd become a great deal less resistant to the idea. And in the meantime, she was happy she wasn't in Wales and that she had her sister close by. As ever, Arabel was easy to please.

As she'd dreamed, Chrystabel would be living at Tremayne Castle when Joseph's Tudor gardens bloomed in the summer. But she hadn't dared to dream of being just a mile from her siblings. While they'd always treasure fond memories of their old life at Grosmont Grange, Chrystabel knew they'd make even better memories in their new homes. It was a fresh start for all three of them, and one they'd sorely needed.

"...so long as ye both shall live?" the vicar concluded expectantly.

In the hush that followed, Chrystabel drew a deep breath. "I will," she pledged, her voice ringing clear and true through the sanctuary.

A few more words, a family heirloom ring slid onto her finger, and she was astonished to find she felt married, the new Viscountess Tremayne.

She felt married. Before the wedding breakfast.

It was, quite definitely, the most wonderful feeling ever.

When Joseph lowered his lips to meet hers, Arabel burst into applause. Chrystabel didn't allow Joseph to kiss her for long, because they were in a church, after all. She wanted to get him alone so they could kiss properly—well, *improperly*—as husband and wife for the first time, but that would have to wait until they were back at Tremayne.

When he released her, she saw that Matthew and Creath had been kissing as well. And that Arabel was grinning at them like a lunatic, clearly overjoyed for both her siblings.

Chrystabel saw that Lady Trentingham—no, make that *Mother*—looked thrilled.

And that Lord Trentingham looked perplexed.

He'd been looking perplexed a lot lately.

"I still don't understand," he grumbled as they all walked back to Tremayne, looking forward to Chrystabel's masterpiece of a wedding breakfast. "You all met just three days before Christmas. How can it be that four people fell in love so fast?"

Feeling happier than she'd thought possible, Chrystabel linked arms with her new father-in-law. "Obviously, it was a Christmas miracle."

AUTHOR'S NOTE

Dear Reader,

Oliver Cromwell is one of the most controversial figures in British history. Depending upon viewpoint, he's been described as both a regicidal military dictator and a revolutionary hero of liberty. But few people today would support his decision to ban Christmas.

Following the execution of King Charles I in 1649, England was ruled by Parliament. Prior to the end of the English Civil War in September 1651, three months before this story starts, Cromwell had become the country's de facto leader. He was officially Lord Protector from 1653 until his death in 1658.

Cromwell and his fellow Puritans believed that everyone should lead their lives according to a strict interpretation of the Bible. They felt it was their mission to cleanse the country of decadence, and their decrees affected all aspects of society.

They believed that women and girls should dress in a "proper" manner. Dresses that were too colorful were frowned upon, and those that weren't modest were banned outright. Makeup was banned: Puritan soldiers actually scrubbed off makeup seen on women in the streets. The theaters were all shut down. Most sports were banned. Swearing was punished by a fine for the first offense, and repeat offenders could be sent to prison.

But most controversial of all, the Puritans regarded Christmas as a wasteful, "popish" festival that threatened core Christian beliefs. Nowhere, they said, did the Bible claim God wanted Christ's birthday celebrated—and so they set about banning all activities relating to Christmas, including going to church on Christmas Day. Shops and markets were ordered to stay open on December 25, and everyone was expected to go about the day as if Christmas didn't exist.

The government outlawed every last remnant of Christmas merry-making. Christmas carols were banned. Christmas puddings were banned. Christmas decorations were banned. In London, soldiers were ordered to patrol the streets and take, by force if necessary, any food being cooked for a Christmas celebration. The smell of a goose roasting could bring wrath down upon a family.

Like Chrystabel's family, however, many people continued to celebrate in secret. And in not-so-secret, too, especially as the years of Cromwell's Protectorate went on. Semi-clandestine religious services were held on Christmas Day, and the secular elements of the holiday occurred more and more often. On Christmas Day in 1656, Members of Parliament were unhappy because they'd got little sleep the previous night due to the noise of the neighbors' "preparations for this foolish day," and because that morning they had seen "not a shop open, nor a creature stirring" in London. Many writers anonymously argued in print that it was proper to celebrate Christmas and that the government had no right to interfere.

At the Restoration in 1661, when King Charles II returned to claim his throne and all legislation from 1642-60 was declared null and void, Christmas was celebrated with much joy and wide popular support. And it's been that way ever since.

On a much less serious subject: The oldest mulled wine recipes do not have orange or lemon or any other fruit in them. But many modern mulled wine recipes do. I like to think that someone like Joseph might have first tried adding those ingredients!

Most of the homes in my books are modeled on real places you can visit. Tremayne Castle was inspired by Thornbury Castle in Gloucestershire, which is twelve miles from the city of Bristol, just where Joseph's castle is in this story.

Thornbury Castle was built during the reign of Henry VIII, by Edward Stafford, 3rd Duke of Buckingham. But he didn't get to finish it, and he wasn't able to enjoy it for long. At the time, Buckingham was one of few peers with substantial Plantagenet blood, and he felt he should be in line for the throne. After a disgruntled servant betrayed him to the king, he was arrested for treason, tried, and executed on Tower Hill. King Henry claimed the castle for himself and spent ten days there while on his honeymoon tour with Anne Boleyn. It remained royal property until the death of his daughter Mary I, when it was returned to the duke's descendants.

The beautiful Church of St. Mary the Virgin *is* next door to Thornbury Castle, and there used to be a timber bridge connecting them. Although the bridge itself is long since gone, bits of evidence remain.

Is there a priest hole at Thornbury? No one knows for sure, but there are rumors there's one to be found—and several secret panels have been discovered at Thornbury, so it doesn't seem terribly unlikely. On the south side of the castle, part of the outer wall extends in a U-shape that's divided down the middle into two rooms. Curiously, one room is larger than the other, and the suspicion is that there may be a priest hole in the blocked-off space. Thornbury also has a tunnel that starts by the former dungeon (now the wine cellar), runs beneath the courtyard, and comes up by the old castle well.

Thornbury Castle is now a luxurious hotel. Castle accommodations aren't ever inexpensive, but Thornbury's prices are more reasonable than most. If you've ever dreamed of staying at a castle, I highly recommend this one. It is absolutely gorgeous inside, and you might get to stay in Chrystabel's bedroom with the curved oriel windows like I did!

I hope you enjoyed *A Secret Christmas*! If you haven't read the rest of my Chase Family Series, you might want to start with the three books about Chrystabel and Joseph's daughters. The first one is *Violet*. Please read on for an excerpt.

And if you *have* read the rest of my Chase Family Series, you might want to read about descendants of the Chase family—in which case you should check out *Lost in Temptation*, Book 1 in my Regency Chase Family Series. Please read on for an excerpt as well as more bonus material!

Always,

Lauren Royal

ACKNOWLEDGMENTS

My heartfelt thanks:

To Devon Royal, for moral support, fantastic editing, doing stuff for me so I can write, and being the best daughter in the world.

To my BFF, author Glynnis Campbell, for letting me drag her on a cruise to get this book written.

To Jack, Brent, and Blake, for putting up with me being on deadline.

To my Chase Family Readers Group, for their enthusiastic support.

And to all of my readers, for patiently waiting for this story.

Thank you, one and all!

ABOUT LAUREN ROYAL

I decided to become a writer at the age of eight, after winning a "Why My Mother is the Greatest" essay contest and having my entry published in a major newspaper. Seeing my words in print was a thrill! But everyone told me it's too hard for novelists to get published, so after college I spent fourteen years as the CEO of my own jewelry store chain before writing my first book. A mistake? Maybe...but my first heroine, Amethyst, was a jeweler, so at least I took advantage of that wise old saying, "Write what you know." And I learned a good lesson: Don't let other people tell you what you can or can't do!

I write humorous historical romance mostly set in England and Scotland in the 17th and 19th centuries (Restoration and Regency periods). I've been oh-so-lucky to see my books hit bestseller lists all over the world, including the New York Times and USA Today lists, making this second career a real dream come true. I live in Southern California with my husband, our three young adult children, and one constantly shedding cat, and I still think my mother is the greatest!

Read on for an excerpt from

Violet

Book 5 of the *Chase Family Series*
by Lauren Royal

Lady Violet Ashcroft has no plans to marry. Ever. She'd rather be improving her mind than risking her tender heart. But her matchmaking mama is determined to change Violet's mind—and the handsome, intellectual viscount moving in next door might be just the ticket...

~

England
July 15, 1673

S T. SWITHIN'S DAY. Well, it was fitting.

Viscount Lakefield stared out his carriage window at the miserable, wet landscape. According to St. Swithin's legend, if it rained on the fifteenth of July, it would continue for forty days and nights. Normally not a man given to superstition, today Ford Chase found such nonsense plausible.

This was shaping up to be the worst day of his life.

The carriage rattled over the drawbridge and into the modest courtyard of Greystone, his older brother's small castle. Cold rain-drops pelted Ford's head when he shoved open the door and leapt to the circular drive. Drenched gravel crunching beneath his boots, he made his way down a short, covered passageway and banged the knocker on the unassuming oak door.

Benchley cracked open the door, then slipped outside and shut it behind him. "My lord, what brings you here today?"

"I wish to speak with my brother." Ford frowned down at the small, wiry valet. What was he doing answering the door? "Will you be letting me in?"

"I think not." Benchley lifted his beak of a nose. "I'll fetch Lord Greystone." And with that, he disappeared back into the ancient castle.

Shivering, Ford stood frozen in disbelief before deciding this treatment fit in with the rest of his day. Rain dripped from his long brown hair to sprinkle on the stones at his feet. Wondering why he should need permission to enter his brother's home, he moved to reach for the latch.

The door opened, and his brother stepped out. He looked haggard, his face a pasty gray, his green eyes and black hair dull.

"Colin? What the devil's going on?"

"Illness. Measles, we think. Thank God you're here."

Ford pulled his surcoat tighter around himself. "Come again?"

"Amy is ill, along with little Hugh and the baby. And half of the servants. One of them died yesterday," Colin added grimly.

"Died?" Ford's gut twisted as he thought of Amy—Colin's beautiful, raven-haired wife—and their bright four-year-old son, Hugh, and the baby, Aidan...all dead.

"It's not so bad as all that," Colin rushed to assure him, evidently reading the concern on his face. "The poor maid was eighty if she were a day, and the disease went straight to her lungs. I'm not expecting my family to perish."

"At least you won't be getting it. If you'll remember, all four of us had it while in exile on the Continent."

"I could hardly forget." Appearing as though he could barely hold himself up, Colin leaned against the doorpost. "But what does that have to do with now?"

"At a Royal Society lecture, I learned one cannot fall ill with the same disease twice," Ford explained.

"I've had measles more than once."

"Not true measles, the one with the high fever. Spotted skin is a symptom of many different conditions."

"Trust you to know something like that." Although Colin looked relieved, his smile was bleak. "Still, the fever is savage, and Jewel has yet to suffer measles. True measles, as you put it. Will you take her from here before she succumbs as well? It would relieve my mind, and Amy's too, I'm sure. The worry is doing her recovery no good."

Alarm bells went off in Ford's head. Take his niece? Where? What would he do with a young girl? "Well, I only stopped by to let you know I've left London and will be at Lakefield for the foreseeable future—"

"Perfect."

"—working on my new watch design. I...I just wanted to be alone for a while. Lady Tabitha has eloped."

"With the rest of the family off in Scotland, I was at my wit's end deciding what to do. I was about to settle Jewel in the village. But this will be much better—"

"Tabitha *eloped*," Ford repeated, wondering why his brother hadn't reacted to this astonishing news. After all, Tabitha had just upset his entire life plan.

"She eloped?" Colin blinked, then shook his head. "Come now, Ford. What did you expect? After six years of suffering your attentions whenever you deigned to show up in London, and sharing your bed, I assume—"

She had. So what of it? No one in King Charles II's circle was virtuous. Colin hadn't been a monk before meeting his wife, and neither had their oldest brother Jason. The three Chase brothers were all titled and intimates of the king, which naturally meant they were popular with the ladies at court—and none of them had hesitated to take advantage in their day.

"—a lady," Colin continued, "would expect a proposal."

"I *told* her we'd marry someday. In two or three years." Tabitha had seemed the ideal woman for Ford—stunningly beautiful, always ready to attend a ball or an evening at court. They matched well in bed, and when they weren't together she busied herself with whatever women liked to do, leaving him plenty of time for his work. "For heaven's sake, she's only twenty-one, and I'm just twenty-eight. Jason married at thirty-two, and no one was on his back."

"I married at twenty-eight."

"*You* were in a hurry to have children."

"While I'm sure *you* would as soon do without them altogether." Colin rubbed his eyes. "You really have no idea why Tabitha gave up on you, do you? I hate to tell you this, little brother, but it's time you grew up and realized there's more to life than science and seduction. As the baby of the family, maybe Jason and I coddled you too much."

From beyond the passageway, the patter of rain filled their sudden silence. Colin was obviously weary, so Ford thought it best not to argue. Doubtless Colin had spent sleepless nights watching over his wife and sons—exactly why Ford wasn't ready for a family of his own.

"You look tired," he said. "You'd best get some rest."

His brother heaved a sigh. "I'd rest easier if I knew you had Jewel. You'll take her, won't you?"

What the devil would he do with a girl who wasn't yet six? He loved her, of course. She shared his blood. But that didn't mean he had a clue how to care for her. Bouncing her on his knee or playing a simple card game with her was one thing. A few minutes of fun before returning her to her parents. But to be responsible for a child...

He shoved a hand through his wet hair. "For how long?"

"A week or two. Maybe three. Until the illness has run its course." Colin twisted the signet ring on his finger, narrowing his gaze. "Why are you hesitating? I need you."

"I'm not hesitating," Ford protested. "I just..."

His brother's eyes opened wide. "Did you think I'd expect you to care for her on your own? Heaven forbid." His lips quirked as though he might laugh, but he coughed instead. On purpose, Ford was sure. "I'll send Lydia along with her."

Despite his annoyance at being read so easily—not to mention distrusted—the tension left Ford's shoulders. With Lydia, Jewel's very competent nurse, on the premises, he wouldn't have to care for the girl, wouldn't have to struggle to interpret her mystifying female language and needs. He could just poke his head into her room and say hello every once in a while.

"You won't have to do a thing," Colin added, his tight expression easing into a wry half-smile. "You might try talking with your niece, though. It's time you learned to communicate with the lesser species. You know, those of us of insufficient age or intelligence to grasp the deepest secrets of the universe."

"I don't—"

"Maybe *that* was your problem with Tabitha."

Ford gritted his teeth. He'd never fooled himself into thinking he understood the opposite sex. His science was what drove him. But he'd had no problems with Tabitha, and he was finished with this discussion.

"Of course I'll take Jewel," he said, consciously relaxing his jaw. "Bring her out—I'll be waiting in my carriage."

~

"*L*ISTEN TO THIS." Sitting with her two sisters while their mother worked nearby, Violet Ashcroft cleared her throat. "'To say that a blind custom of obedience should be a surer obligation than duty taught and understood...is to affirm that a blind man may tread surer by a guide than a seeing man by a light.'"

"What is that supposed to mean?" her youngest sister, Lily, asked. Busily stitching her tapestry in the grayish light from the large picture window, Lily probably had little real desire to know what the quote meant. But she was unfailingly kind, and Violet would never turn away from anyone willing to listen.

She hitched herself forward on the green brocade chair. "Well, now—"

"Why do you care?" their middle sister, Rose, interrupted. Rose cared little for anything that didn't have to do with dancing, clothes, or men. Looking up from the vase of flowers she was arranging, she tossed her gleaming ringlets. "It's nothing but a bunch of gibberish, if you ask me."

"Nobody asked." Violet pointedly looked to Lily. "Did you hear anyone ask?"

"Girls." Clucking her tongue, their mother poured a dipperful of water into the kettle over the fire. "I used to comfort myself that when you all grew up, this bickering would cease. Yet it never has."

Lily's blue eyes were all innocence, despite having reached the advanced age of sixteen. "But Mum," she said sweetly. Their mother's proper name was Chrystabel, but as their flower-obsessed father

183

called her Chrysanthemum, they'd taken to calling her Mum. "It's loving bickering."

"And a bad example for your young brother." With a sigh, Chrystabel resumed plucking petals from a bunch of lush pink roses. "What *does* it mean?" she asked Violet. "And who said it?"

"It means we should understand why we are doing things instead of blindly following orders. Rather like our Ashcroft family motto: *Interroga Conformationem*, Question Convention. But said much more eloquently, don't you think? By Francis Bacon."

Violet snapped the book closed, its title, *Advancement of Learning*, winking gold from the spine in her lap. "But I'm wondering," she teased. "When did *my* Mum become interested in philosophy?"

"I'm interested in all my children's hobbies."

"Philosophy is more than a hobby," Violet protested. "It's a way of looking at life."

"Of course it is." The kettle was bubbling merrily, spewing steam into the dim room. The fire and a few candles were no match for this gloomy, rainy afternoon. "Will you come and hold this for me, dear?"

Violet set down the book and wandered over to the large, utilitarian table she always thought looked somewhat out of place in what used to be a formal drawing room. "Did Father bring you more roses this morning?"

"Doesn't he always?" Chrystabel's musical laughter warmed Violet to her toes. "Sweet man, he is, rising early to gather them between dawn and sunrise, when their scent is at its peak."

Violet's laughter joined her mother's. "Insane man, you mean." *Sweet* wasn't a word she'd use to describe the Earl of Trentingham —*eccentric* fit her father much better. But her parents both seemed to be blind where the other's oddities were concerned.

Not that that was a bad thing. For certain, if Violet were ever to wed—an event she considered unlikely indeed—her husband would have to be more than a little bit blind. She didn't have rich chestnut hair like her sisters—hers was a blander, lighter brown. And her eyes were plain brown as well, not the mysterious almost-black of Rose's or the fathomless deep-blue of Lily's. Just brown.

Average, she decided. Neither fat nor thin. Not tall like Rose nor petite like Lily, but medium height. Average.

But, happily, she didn't mind being average. Because average was rarely noticed, and the truth was, she'd never liked being the center of attention.

Rose thrived on it, though. "Let me help, Mum," she squealed, dropping the stem of blue sweet peas she'd been about to add to her floral arrangement. "Violet probably won't get the top on straight."

Tactless, at best, but at seventeen, Rose still had some time to grow up. With an indulgent sigh, Violet stuck a wooden block upright in the big bowl. She held it in place while Mum sprinkled in all the rose petals, then turned to lift the kettle.

In a slow, careful stream, Chrystabel poured just enough water over the fragrant flowers to cover them. Quickly Rose popped another, larger bowl upside down on top of the wooden block, using it as a pedestal. The steam would collect beneath and drip down the edges to the tray below. As it cooled, it would separate into rosewater and essential rose oil.

Distillation, Mum called it.

A rich, floral scent wafted up, and Violet inhaled deeply. As hobbies went, she did appreciate her mother's unusual one of perfume-making.

"Thank you, girls," Chrystabel said when Violet released the bowl. "Would you hand me that vial of lavender essence?"

Violet turned and squinted at the labels, then reached for the proper glass tube. "I read in the news sheet this morning that Christopher Wren is going to be knighted later this year. And he was just elected to the Council of the Royal Society."

Mum took the vial. "That odd group of scientists?"

Violet smiled inside, thinking Chrystabel Ashcroft a bit odd herself. "There are philosophers as members, too. And statesmen and physicians. I'd love to hear one of their lectures someday."

"The Royal Society doesn't allow women at their meetings." Chrystabel pulled the cork stopper and waved the lavender under her nose. "Besides, most of the men are married."

"I don't want them to court me, Mum." On the whole, she didn't want anyone to court her, much to her mother's distress. "I only wish to cudgel their brains."

Frowning, Chrystabel lowered a dropper into the vial. "Cudgel their—"

"Talk to them, I mean. Share some ideas. They're so brilliant."

"Men aren't interested in *talking* to women," Rose told her, "and the sooner you learn that, the sooner you'll find one of your own."

"Faith, Rose. I'm only twenty. You'd think I was in my dotage, the way you've become set on marrying me off."

"You're expected to wed before I do."

The words were uttered so innocently, Violet couldn't find it in her to hold a grudge. Of course Rose wanted to marry, and convention dictated the girls wed in order.

But Violet was nothing if not realistic. She knew her plain looks, together with her unusual interests, were likely to make it difficult—if not impossible—for her to find a compatible husband. But that didn't really bother her, and she would never want her own dim prospects to keep her lovely sisters from finding happiness.

Besides, when had the Ashcrofts been conventional? They could marry in any order they chose. Or in her case, not at all.

She watched her mother add three drops of lavender to the bottle of fragrance she was creating, then swirl it carefully.

"Is that a new blend?" Violet asked.

"For Lady Cunningham." Chrystabel sniffed deeply and passed the bottle to her oldest daughter. "What do you think?"

Violet smelled it and considered. "Too sweet. Lady Cunningham is anything but sweet." The woman's voice could curdle milk. Violet handed back the mixture, hunting for the vial of petitgrain she knew would soften it.

Nodding approvingly, her mother added two drops, then made a note on the little recipe card she kept for each of her friends.

"Look," Lily said, her embroidery forgotten. She rose and settled herself in the large, green-padded window seat. "There's a carriage about to pass by."

Chrystabel and Rose hurried to join her at window, while Violet returned to her chair and opened her book. "So?"

"So..." Lily brushed her fingers over one of the flower arrangements that Rose left all over the house, sending a burst of scent into the air. "We get so little traffic here, I'm just wondering who it might be."

"The three of you are too curious for your own good." Violet flipped a page, hoping to find another sage insight. Not that she'd bother sharing it this time.

"It's our occasional neighbor," her mother said. "The viscount."

Violet's attention strayed from Bacon's brilliance. "How do you know?"

"I recognize his carriage. A hand-me-down from his brother, the marquess."

"How is it you know everyone's business?" Violet wondered aloud.

"It's not so very difficult, my dear. One need only take an interest, open her eyes and ears, and use her head. I believe the viscount is in tight straits. Not only because of the second-hand carriage, but heavens, the state of his gardens. Your father nearly chokes every time we ride past."

"I'm surprised Father hasn't made his way over to set the garden to rights," Lily said.

"Don't think he hasn't considered it." Chrystabel leaned her palms on the windowsill, studying the passing coach. "Why, I do believe Lord Lakefield isn't alone."

Despite herself, Violet rose, one finger holding her place in the book. "And how do you know that?"

"The vehicle's curtains aren't drawn." Chrystabel gave a happy gasp of discovery. "There's a child inside! And a woman!"

Her interest finally piqued, Violet wandered to the window to see, but of course the carriage was only a blur.

Everything more than a few feet from Violet's eyes always looked like a blur. It was the reason she preferred staying at home with her books and news sheets, rather than going about to socialize with her mother and two younger sisters. She was afraid she'd embarrass herself by failing to recognize a friend across the room.

"Well, well, well," Mum said. "I must go bring the lady a gift of perfume and welcome her to the neighborhood."

"You mean find out who she is," Violet said.

Her mother's second hobby was delivering perfume and receiving gossip in exchange. Not that anyone begrudged her the information. To the contrary, Chrystabel Ashcroft never needed to pry a word out of anyone. Warm and well-loved, she barely walked in the door before women began spilling their secrets.

On the rare occasions her mother had succeeded in dragging her along, Violet had seen it happen, her bad eyes notwithstanding.

"I wonder if the viscount has married?" Rose asked.

"I expect not," Chrystabel said. "He's much too intellectual for anyone I know." As the carriage disappeared into the distance, she turned from the window. "Why, he's a member of that Royal Society, isn't he?"

"I believe so." Violet watched her mother wander back to the table, wishing she'd never mentioned wanting to attend a Royal Society lecture. The last thing she needed was Mum plotting her marriage. "Perhaps he would suit Rose or Lily."

"I think not." Mum sniffed the perfume in progress, then chose another vial. "I cannot imagine whom he would suit, but certainly not your sisters."

"It's just as well," Rose said, "since you know we three have a pact to save one another from your matchmaking schemes."

It was one thing—perhaps the only thing—the sisters agreed on.

"Heavens, girls. It's not as though I arrange marriages behind the backs of my friends." *Everyone* Chrystabel knew was her friend. Literally. And they all adored her. "All of my brides and grooms are willing—"

"Victims?" Violet broke in to supply.

"Participants," Chrystabel countered.

Lily sat and retrieved her handiwork. "How many weddings have you arranged this year, Mum? Three? Four?"

"Five," their mother said with not a little pride. She tapped her fingernails on the vial. "Only seven months in, and a banner year already. But none, I assure you, against the participants' will."

Rose plopped back onto her own chair. "You're not matching me up, Mum. I can find my own husband."

"Me, too," Lily said.

"Me three," Violet added.

"Of course you all can." Chrystabel's graceful fingers stilled. "I wouldn't dream of meddling in my own daughters' lives."

~

AVAILABLE NOW!

Learn more about *Violet* at www.LaurenRoyal.com

Read on for an excerpt from

Lost in Temptation

Book 1 of the *Regency Chase Family Series*
by Lauren Royal

Lady Alexandra Chase has always done what was expected of her. But when the man she's loved since her girlhood returns from a long spell abroad, she quite suddenly finds herself hoping the fine lord her brother has picked for her *won't* propose.

⤳

Cainewood Castle, the South of England
Summer 1808

*I*T WAS ALMOST like touching him.

Lady Alexandra Chase usually sketched a profile in just a few minutes, but she took her time today, lingering over the experience in the darkened room. Standing on one side of a large, framed pane of glass while Tristan sat sideways on the other, she traced his shadow cast by the glow of a candle. Her pencil followed his strong chin, his long, straight nose, the wide slope of his forehead, capturing his image on the sheet of paper she'd tacked to her side of the glass. Noticing a stray lock that tumbled down his brow, she hesitated, wanting to make certain she caught it just right.

Someone walked by the open door, causing Tris's shadow to flicker as the candle wavered. "Are you finished yet?" he asked from behind the glass panel.

"Hold still," she admonished, resisting the urge to peek around at him. "Artistry requires patience."

"This is a profile, not oil on canvas."

True, and she often wished she had the talent to paint, like her youngest sister, Corinna. But the fact that she was missing something Corinna had—that elusive, innate ability to see things others missed and convey them in color, light, and shade—didn't keep her from taking pride in her own hobby.

Alexandra made excellent profile portraits.

She'd been asking Tris to sit for her for years, but he'd never seemed to find time before. "You promised you'd sit still," she reminded him, knowing better than to read malice into his comment. "Just this once before you leave."

"I'm sitting," he said, and although his profile remained immobile, she could hear the laughter in his voice.

She loved that evidence of his control, just like she loved everything about Tris Nesbitt.

She'd been eight when they first met. Her favorite brother, Griffin, had brought him home between terms at school. In the many years since, as he and Griffin completed Eton and then Oxford, Tris had visited often, claiming to prefer his friend's large family to the quiet home he shared with his father.

Alexandra couldn't remember when she'd fallen in love, but she felt like she'd loved Tris forever.

Of course, nothing would ever come of it. Now, at fifteen, she was practical enough to accept that her father, the formidable Marquess of Cainewood, would never allow her to marry plain Mr. Tristan Nesbitt.

But that didn't stop her from wishing she could. It didn't stop her stomach from tingling when she heard his low voice, didn't stop her heart from skipping when she felt herself caught in his intense, silver-gray gaze.

Not that he directed his gaze her way often. It wasn't that he was unfriendly, but, after all, as far as he was concerned she was little more than Griffin's pesky younger sister.

Knowing Tris couldn't see her now, she skimmed her fingertips over his shadow, wishing she were touching *him* instead. She'd never touched him, not in real life. Such intimacy simply didn't occur between young ladies and men. Most especially between a marquess's daughter and an untitled man's son.

The drawing room's draperies were shut, and the resulting dimness seemed to afford them an odd closeness alone in the room. She traced the flow of his cravat illuminated through the glass onto her paper. "Where are you going again?" she asked, although she knew.

"Jamaica. My uncle wishes me to look after his interests. He owns a plantation there; I'm to learn how it's run."

He sounded sad. During this visit he'd seemed sad quite a bit. "Is that what you wish to do with your life?"

"He doesn't mean for me to stay there permanently. Only to acquaint myself with the operation so I can make intelligent decisions from afar."

"But do you wish to become his man of business? Do you want to manage his properties? Or would you rather do something else?"

He shrugged, his profile tilting, then settling back into the lines she'd so carefully drawn. "He financed my entire education. Have I a choice?"

"I suppose not." Her choices were limited, too. "How long will you be gone?"

"A year at the least, probably two, perhaps three."

Everything was changing. Griffin would leave soon as well—their father had bought him a commission in the cavalry. Although Griffin and Tris had spent much of the past few years at school and university, these new developments seemed different. They'd be across oceans. It wasn't that Alexandra would be alone—she'd still have her parents and her grandmother, her oldest brother and her two younger sisters—but she was already feeling the loss.

"Two or three years," she echoed, knowing Griffin would likely be gone even longer. "That seems a lifetime."

Tris's image shimmied as he laughed out loud. "I expect it might, to one as young as you."

He wasn't that much older, only one-and-twenty. But she supposed he'd seen a lot in the extra six years he had on her. Young men left home as adolescents to pursue their educations. They spent time hunting at country houses and carousing about London.

While she didn't exactly chafe at her own more restrictive life, she was counting the years and months until she'd turn eighteen and have her first season. She'd spent hour upon hour imagining the balls, the parties, and all the eligible young lords. One of those titled men would be her entrée to a new life as a society wife. A more exciting life, she

LAUREN ROYAL

hoped. And she would love her husband, she was certain, although right now she could hardly imagine loving any man besides Tris.

He'd never indicated any interest in her, but of course he wouldn't. As well as she, Tris knew his place. But that didn't stop her from wishing she knew whether he cared.

Just whether or not he cared.

"Will you bring me something from Jamaica?" she asked, startling herself with her boldness.

"Like what?" She heard astonishment in his voice. "A pineapple or some sugarcane?"

It was her turn to laugh. "Anything. Surprise me."

"All right, then. I will." He fell silent a moment, as though trying to commit the promise to memory. "Are you finished yet?"

"For now." She set down her pencil and walked to the windows, drew back the draperies, and blinked. The room's familiar blue-and-coral color scheme suddenly seemed too bright.

She turned toward him, reconciling his face with the profile she'd just sketched. From the boy she'd met years ago, he'd grown into a handsome, masculine man—one might even say he looked arresting. But she wouldn't describe him as pretty. His jaw was too strong, his mouth too wide, his brows too heavy and straight. As she watched, he raked a hand through his hair—tousled, streaky dark blond hair that always seemed just a bit too long.

Her fingers itched to run through it, to sweep the stray lock from his forehead.

"It will take me a while to complete the portrait," she told him as she walked back to where he sat beside the glass, "but I'll have it ready for you before you leave."

"Keep it for me."

She blew out the candle, leaning close enough to catch a whiff of his scent, smelling soap and starch and something uniquely Tris. "Don't you want it?"

He rose from the chair, smiling down at her from his greater height. "I'll probably lose it if I take it with me."

"Very well, then." She'd been hoping he'd say she should keep it to

196

remember him by. But as always, Tris was the perfect gentleman. If he did harbor any affection for her, he wouldn't betray so with such a remark. "I wish you a safe journey, Mr. Nesbitt."

She'd called him Tristan—or Tris—for years now, but suddenly that seemed too informal.

His gray gaze remained steady. "Thank you, Lady Alexandra. I wish you a happy life."

A happy life. She could be married by the time he returned, she realized with a shock. In fact, if he were gone three years, she very likely would be.

Her heart sank at the thought.

But at least she'd have his profile. When she was finished, it would be black on white in an elegant oval frame, a perfect likeness of his face. And she'd almost touched him while making it.

As he walked from the room, she peeled the paper off the glass and hugged it to her chest.

~

RATAFIA PUFFS

Take halfe a pound of Ground Almonds and a little more than that of Sugar. Make it up in a stiff paste with Whites of five Eggs and a little Essence of Almond whipt to a Froth. Beat it all well in a Mortar, and make it up in little Loaves, then bake them in a very cool oven on Paper and Tin-Plates.

I call these my magical sweets...my husband proposed directly after eating only one!

—Eleanor, Marchioness of Cainewood, 1728

Cainewood Castle, seven years later
June 1815

"*N*OT ALL OF IT!" Alexandra Chase made a mad grab for her youngest sister's arm. "We're instructed to add a *little* more sugar than almonds."

Corinna stopped grating and frowned. "I *like* sugar."

"You won't like these ratafia puffs if they're *all* sugar," their middle sister, Juliana, said as she took the cone-shaped sugar loaf and set it on the scarred wooden table in the center of Cainewood Castle's cavernous kitchen.

"Here, my arm is tired." Alexandra handed Corinna the bowl of egg whites she'd been beating, then scooped a proper amount of the sugar and poured it into another bowl that held the ground almonds. Stirring them together, she shook her head at Corinna. "You really are quite hopeless with recipes. If you didn't look so much like Mama, I'd wonder if you're truly her child."

A sudden sheen of tears brightened Corinna's brilliant blue eyes. She quickly blinked them away. "She always made good sweets, didn't she?"

"Excellent sweets," Juliana said in a sympathetic tone, shooting a warning glance to her older sister.

Alexandra felt abashed and maybe a little teary herself. She looked away, her gaze wandering the whitewashed stone walls of the kitchen. Heaven knew Corinna was the most talented of the three of them. She'd meant only to tease her sister about her lack of their family's renowned skills for making sweets, not remind her of their mother. Memories could still be painful, since Mama had been gone less than two years.

But the time for sadness was over...following years of mourning various family members one after another, Alexandra and her sisters were finally wearing cheerful colors and ready to face the world. In Alexandra's case, she was *more* than ready to put the sorrow behind her and get on with her life.

During her first and only season four long years ago, she'd entertained many excellent offers of marriage. But when her grandmother died shortly thereafter, all thoughts of a wedding had been postponed, and she'd missed the 1812 season while mourning her. Then her father had died, and she'd missed the 1813 season while mourning him. Then her mother had died, and she'd missed the 1814 season while mourning her. Then her oldest brother had died, making 1815's season yet another one of solitude here in the countryside.

All of the marriage-minded men who'd courted her had long since found available brides. But Alexandra wasn't sure she wanted to face another season, with all the attending games and frivolity. She just wanted to be a wife. She wanted to put her old life behind her and start over in a new place and a new situation.

As for her younger sisters, they'd yet to be presented at court and were beside themselves at the thought of finally having a season. It seemed all Juliana and Corinna could talk of were the many parties, balls, breakfasts, dances, and soirees they were looking forward to attending.

"I can hardly wait for next spring," Corinna said, echoing Alexandra's musings.

Juliana added a few drops of almond extract to the egg whites. "If Griffin has his way, we'll all be married long before spring. We'll *never* have a season."

"He cannot get us all married off so quickly." Alexandra idly stirred the almonds and sugar. "Never mind that he's been inviting his friends here to meet us since before we were out of mourning. You two will have your seasons. He'll have to be content with my marriage for now."

"If the 'magical' ratafia puffs do their job." Corinna handed the bowl of eggs back to Alexandra. "Here, now *my* arm is tired. This is hard work." Mopping her forehead with a towel, she looked pointedly through an archway to where a scullery maid stood drying a towering stack of dishes. "I cannot understand why you won't ask *her*—"

"If the magic is to work," Juliana interrupted patiently, "Alexandra must make the ratafia puffs herself, not relegate the task to a servant."

"Holy Hannah!" Corinna tossed her mane of long, wavy brown hair, which she insisted on wearing down even though she had long since become old enough to put it up. "It's blazing hot in here with the coal burning all the day long. Ladies don't work in the kitchen."

Still beating the eggs, Alexandra glanced at the ancient, stained journal that lay open on the long table. "Chase ladies do. Our foremothers have been making sweets forever." The heirloom volume was filled with recipes penned by Chase females going all the way back to the seventeenth century. "It's a tradition," she added, looking back up at her sister. "Will you be the first to break it?"

"Perhaps. Unlike you, I don't put much stock in tradition."

Alexandra beat the eggs harder. "You should—"

"Girls." Always the peacemaker, Juliana took the bowl of stiffened eggs and dumped the almond and sugar mixture into it. "Why is there no ratafia in ratafia puffs?" she asked, adeptly changing the subject.

"Perhaps we're supposed to serve ratafia with them," Corinna suggested.

Alexandra laughed. "Griffin invited Lord Shelton to take tea, not to drink spirits. I expect they're called ratafia puffs because they taste of almonds like ratafia does."

Corinna dipped a finger into the sweet mixture and licked it off. "Do you think Lord Shelton will really propose?"

Juliana rolled her lovely hazel eyes. "Alexandra could feed him dirt and he'd propose. Have you not seen the way he looks at her?"

"Like he'd rather eat her than the sweets?"

"Oh, do hold your tongues." Alexandra *had* noticed the way Lord Shelton looked at her, and although she couldn't figure out *why* he looked at her that way—she knew she had a pretty face, but her boring brown eyes and impossible-to-control brown hair left a lot to be desired—she had to confess it was gratifying. She only wished she felt the same way about him.

But even though he didn't make her heart race, he was handsome and kind. He possessed a fortune of his own, so she knew he wasn't after her sizable dowry. And he lived nearby, so she would see her sisters often.

He really was quite perfect.

Once, at fifteen, she'd basked in the illusion of love. But now she suspected love to be an unrealistic, childish expectation. Years of sadness and disappointment had taught her to expect less than she used to of life.

With any luck, the ratafia puffs would work their magic, she thought as she dropped shiny dollops of the batter onto a paper-lined tin baking sheet.

The Chase sisters were long overdue for some luck.

~

FOR THE FIRST time in seven years, Tristan rode over Cainewood Castle's drawbridge and into its quadrangle. As a groom hurried from the stables, he swung down from his black gelding, his gaze skimming the clipped lawn and the four stories of living quarters that formed a U around it.

Cainewood didn't look any different, although there was no reason it should. If he remembered right, the castle had been in Chase hands—save during the Commonwealth—for close to six hundred years. He shouldn't have expected it to change in the last seven.

But *he'd* changed, so it felt odd that this place hadn't.

Seven years ago, he'd been a young man of one-and-twenty on his way to Jamaica to begin a promising career working with his generous Uncle Harold. He'd had a new degree from the University of Oxford, a soon-to-be-healed broken heart, and nary a serious care in the world.

Four years ago, Uncle Harold had died, and Tristan had taken his place as the Marquess of Hawkridge.

These days, he was anything but carefree.

The young groom tipped his cap. "Take your horse, my lord?"

"Yes, thank you." Tristan handed over the reins. As his mount was led away, his gaze wandered the ancient keep—still as tumbledown as he remembered it—and past it to the old tilting yard that lay beyond. He smiled, recalling games played there as a youth, he and Griffin— and often, Griffin's charming little sisters—running through the untamed, ankle-high vegetation. Those summers spent here during his school years were memories to be treasured. Griffin's family had been a jolly substitute for the lack of his own.

"Tristan. Or I suppose I should call you Hawkridge. Whichever, it's been entirely too long."

Lost in his thoughts, he hadn't heard Griffin approach, but now he turned to see his old friend holding out a hand. He reached his own to grasp it.

"Ah, hell," Griffin said and pulled him into a rough embrace instead.

Tristan tensed for a stunned moment. Other than the impersonal attentions of his valet or a perfunctory handshake now and then, it was the first human touch he had felt in...entirely too long to remember.

He clapped his friend on the back. "Yes. Entirely too long," he echoed as he drew away. "Am I supposed to call you Cainewood?"

"Strikes the ear wrong after all these years, doesn't it?" Like the castle, Griffin's slightly crooked smile was familiar. "Griffin will do. I didn't expect you until tomorrow at the earliest."

Tristan walked with him toward the entrance. "Your note sounded urgent."

Before they reached the front steps, the double oak doors opened. Cainewood's longtime butler stood between them. "Welcome back, my lord," he said with a little bow.

"Why, thank you, Boniface," Tristan returned, pleased to see him again. The man was aptly named, for he had a bonnie face—a youthful countenance that belied his forty-odd years. No matter how hard he tried to look stiff and serious, he never quite succeeded. And other than a touch of gray gracing his temples, the years hadn't changed him a bit.

Tristan couldn't say the same for Griffin. "You look older," he said as they climbed the steps. Griffin's jaw looked firmer; his green eyes looked somewhat world-weary. "But I expect one could say the same of me."

Griffin nodded. "We're both shouldering responsibilities we never thought to have."

"Feeling overburdened, are you?" Tristan was surprised. "Surely the marquessate is less stressful than plotting war strategy."

"You have no idea." They stepped inside. "I have three sisters to marry off, and that's only the beginning—"

"They cannot already be old enough to wed!"

Griffin's laugh boomed through the three-story-high entrance hall, all the way up to its stone-vaulted ceiling. "You expect we aged while time stood still for them?" He led Tristan up the carved stone staircase. "Corinna—the baby—is nearly twenty. Plenty old enough to find a husband."

Tristan frowned. "And Juliana and Alexandra?" he asked, deliberately mentioning her last.

Maybe she would seem less important that way.

"Twenty-one and twenty-two." They turned on the landing and went up a second level to the family's private apartments. "Four deaths in the family have kept them from the marriage mart, but I mean to see them all settled now—and soon."

Griffin ushered Tristan into a dark wood study. Waving him into a leather wing chair, he went to open a cabinet.

Tristan sat warily. "Look, old man, I sympathize with your problem, but your letter indicated you were in dire straits and needed my expertise—"

"Yes." Rather than sitting behind the massive mahogany desk, Griffin chose the chair beside Tristan's. "I appreciate your response." He set two crystal glasses on the small table between them, unstoppered a matching decanter, and began pouring. "Regardless of the fact that you've hidden yourself away in the countryside all these years, you are known far and wide—"

"I'm not in search of a wife!"

"—for your advances in scientific agriculture and land management." In the midst of handing Tristan a glass, Griffin blinked. "Wife? Do you imagine I asked you here to marry one of my sisters? Perish the thought!"

Tristan breathed deep of the brandy as he wavered between relief and annoyance. Never mind that he had no interest in wedding any of Griffin's sisters—or anyone else, for that matter—he wasn't sure he appreciated having his unsuitability thrown directly into his face. "Why did you summon me, then?"

"I need your help. I've heard you've worked miracles with Hawkridge's vineyard."

"I've managed to revive it, yes. We've had two excellent harvests—the wine from last year's is particularly good." Relaxing back, Tristan took a bracing sip of the fine spirits. "You're in need of wine?"

Griffin's sip was more like a gulp. "Charles," he said, referring to his late older brother, "had taken up growing grapes, with an eye to making wine. He planted vines some three years ago—"

"Charles wanted to make wine?"

"It's the latest thing; haven't you heard? What with the prices soaring during the war against France, I suspect he thought to make a killing. But regardless, Charles always was a swell of the first stare."

"Yes," Tristan said dryly. "He was." He well remembered Charles, a tall, dark man with an air of superiority and an eye to owning the best. "Go on, then."

"I've been told not to expect a yield suited for production for another year at the least. But the vines should be bearing fruit by now, shouldn't they? They're not producing anything."

"Three years with nothing at all? Not even the odd bloom?"

"Nothing beyond leaves. I fear they may be dying. And I haven't the foggiest idea what to do." Griffin's fingers tightened on his glass. "I'm trained to lead men into battle, not manage land and livestock."

"Not to mention make wine, which is another enterprise entirely." Tristan sipped thoughtfully. "With more than thirteen thousand acres, a good percentage of that productive, you cannot stand to lose the vineyard? This is your emergency?"

Griffin colored. "I apologize if my letter made it sound dire. But… this was Charles's pet project. He invested a fair amount of funds, and I wish to make a success of it." After hesitating a moment, he met Tristan's eyes. "I hate to think I might fail where my brother would have succeeded. I'm not comfortable with these responsibilities—they were meant to be his, and I wasn't raised to the task. But I mean to make the best of it."

The admission sounded pained, but Tristan could sympathize. He didn't imagine that military officers sat around at night baring their souls. And as for himself, it had been a long time since he'd had anyone to confide in.

"I understand," he said. He hadn't been raised with expectations of inheriting a title, either. Quite the contrary, he'd been born the son of a second son, a mere mister who'd attended the right schools only on the largesse of his uncle. "I'm trying to make the best of my life, too."

Griffin nodded, looking uneasy.

These days, most everyone was uneasy around Tristan.

"Shall I have a look at your vineyard?" He drained his glass, set it down, and began to rise.

"It will have to wait until tomorrow." Waving him back down, Griffin refilled their glasses. "It's a good hour each way by horseback, and I'm expecting another caller shortly. A very acceptable suitor for Alexandra's hand."

Alexandra. Tristan pictured long dark curls and innocent young eyes. He wondered how she'd look all grown up.

He wondered if she'd have the same effect on him she used to.

"We'll ride over in the morning," Griffin added. "You'll stay, won't you? At least long enough to evaluate the situation?"

"I'll stay as long as I'm needed." Though Griffin's problem wasn't as pressing as Tristan had imagined, it had been a long time since he'd felt needed.

And a long time since he'd seen Lady Alexandra Chase.

∼

AVAILABLE NOW!
Learn more about *Lost in Temptation* at www.LaurenRoyal.com

ENTER FOR A CHANCE TO WIN
Chrystabel's sterling silver lion crest pendant!*

Visit the Contest page on Lauren's website
at www.LaurenRoyal.com
and answer a question to be
entered in the monthly drawing.

No purchase necessary. See complete rules on the site.

*Please note: Depending on when you enter, the prize may be another piece of jewelry associated with one of Lauren's books. The author reserves the right to discontinue this promotion at any time.

CONTACT INFORMATION

Email

Lauren@LaurenRoyal.com

Website

www.LaurenRoyal.com

Newsletter

littl.ink/LaurensNews

Facebook Group

facebook.com/groups/ChaseFamilyReaders

Facebook Page

facebook.com/LaurenRoyal

Twitter

twitter.com/readLaurenRoyal

Pinterest

pinterest.com/LaurenRoyal

Made in the USA
Lexington, KY
20 October 2017